Dear Jane, Love Daisy

ESTELLE MAHER

Dear Jane, Love Daisy X

First published by Winged Ribbon Publishing in 2023
Produced by TAUK Publishing
Copyright © 2023 Estelle Maher

ISBN: 978-1-7396388-1-8

To my sister, Alex.
How our lives changed with an email…

"When one of us shines, all of us shine."

— Moira Rose on friendship,
Schitt's Creek, S3 Ep.13

Monday, 13th April

She checked her small, black, sequinned clutch bag one last time for the key card before she was satisfied she could shut the door to her cabin. Of all the things she thought she would panic over on this cruise, it was locking herself out that caused her the most anguish.

This was the first holiday Daisy had been on where she was responsible for the card, a task usually assigned to her late husband, James. He was the organised one. He was the one who booked where they were going, and while Daisy was always grateful for the holiday, she secretly wished he would consult her and ask her what she fancied. She once broached the subject of them taking a cruise, something that she had often daydreamed about.

"Did you see what happened to Leonard DiCaprio?" he protested.

"That was a bloody film!"

"The *Titanic* was a real ship. People died!"

"Well, Leonard Di Caprio wasn't one of them. He might've gone down with the ship, but he soon bobbed back up to go to the Oscars," she said, laughing.

"It's no laughing matter. Plenty to see on dry land, and we'll get there on a plane."

After that, she never offered a suggestion and often reminded herself that she was luckier than a lot of other women. She'd seen most of Benidorm and a fair bit of Torremolinos, which was more than her older sister, Ruth. Ruth had married a man who thought a full day was getting dressed and venturing to the bookie's. With what turned out to be the final wage packet Colin had collected before deciding he didn't want to work anymore, he'd bought an Eternal Beau dinner set, which, the last time Daisy had visited, was still being used. Much of it was chipped, but most of the service remained intact, suggesting Colin had never washed the dishes. When Daisy once enquired to her sister did he ever help her clean the house, Ruth had laughed and said she would be surprised if Colin ever cleaned himself.

Daisy caught herself shuddering at the memory of Colin in his shiny tracksuit, smelling, for some reason, of Bovril. She shuddered and shoved the image from her mind and made her way, for the last time, to the dining room. Tonight was the gala dinner, and formal dress was required. James would be turning in his grave, knowing the £200 dress she wore tonight might never be worn again. But she didn't care now. He was gone, and so was his opinion. She missed him; that was only natural after thirty-five years of marriage, but once she got over his sudden heart attack and the fear of being alone, she soon realised that there was still a lot of Daisy to discover, which excited her. James was only fifty-nine when he died, leaving her devastated. Time didn't help her heal; it just made her get used to him not being there. She was fine food shopping for herself and lying in the middle of the bed. But now she was nearing her sixties, and the person she knew least in the world was herself. In the eighteen months since James had gone, she'd discovered she quite liked the person that was emerging.

When she arrived at the dining room, she was greeted by Carl. He'd been there every night to welcome her.

"Daisy, Daisy, Daisy." He moved from behind the maître d' stand to embrace her. Daisy knew he was teasing. He was more than half her age, though judging by his antics the previous night with the widow from cabin H4, Daisy suspected that was more of an issue to her than Carl. "You are a vision."

"Behave!" She gave him a light swipe with her handbag, and he giggled at her trying to scold him. "Is Jane here?" she asked, changing the subject.

"She is. If you wait one moment, I'll have one of the waiters take you over."

"Oh, don't be daft. I'm more than capable of walking over to the far side of the room."

He nodded, stepped aside and, with a dramatic sweep of his arm, gestured for her to pass. She did so, turning to look over her shoulder at him.

"Hey, Carl, how do I look?" She knew the answer already. She looked good—well, for a woman of her age. Yes, the menopause had thickened her waist, and she'd always wished she was taller than her five-foot-four frame. But she'd held on to her blonde hair for longer than most, and her skin wasn't as lined as others of her age. Plus, she knew how to smile and make others smile too.

"Bellissimo." He placed all his fingers on his lips and blew her a kiss. She smiled and found her swagger as she walked across the restaurant. She might not be the prettiest, the thinnest or the youngest in the room, but she felt pretty, and if anyone happened to be watching her, she'd make sure they got the full benefit of her sexy strut. She'd never lost the art of that.

She spied Jane at their usual table. She'd known Jane for a whole twelve days. They'd met each other in this very dining room after Carl asked them if they'd mind sharing a table with other diners. They'd both agreed and ended up sitting opposite each other and sharing a table with a Texan, who talked incessantly about Ronald Reagan, and the widow from cabin H4. Neither Jane nor Daisy could remember her name and had simply referred to her as H4.

Jane spied her friend approaching and broke into a broad smile. Her physique was a lot slimmer than Daisy's—rakish, one could call it—and her hair was dark. Daisy suspected the colour was from a tube and applied by someone named Allesandro or Valentino. She wondered what Jane's ex-husband was like and how much he'd changed her. Jane gave off an air of confidence, of being strong and assertive, but then would suddenly become unsure and nervous. Far too often, Daisy glimpsed a broken woman who tried to mask her disappointments by changing the subject.

Was she always like that, or was it the result of circumstance? Which was the true Jane? Maybe even Jane didn't know.

As Jane stood, Daisy noticed she, too, was wearing a black dress. However, Jane's was very plain and simple. For a moment, Daisy thought of Camilla Parker Bowles.

"Daisy, my darling." Jane opened her arms and scooped her friend in for a kiss on the cheek. "You look so…sparkly," she finally decided to say.

Daisy wasn't sure that this was a compliment.

"And you look so…smart." Daisy regretted her choice of adjective, a word better suited for when you were going to an interview, but when she saw Jane smiling and smoothing her dress in agreement, she breathed a sigh of relief.

"Thank you, Daisy. I actually bought this dress when my mother died, but it's from L.K. Bennett, and it seemed a shame not to give it another outing."

Daisy looked Jane over again and agreed to herself that it was indeed a dress to mourn in. Even if you only wanted to mourn the lack of a coloured button.

They had the table to themselves this evening—they hadn't shared their table with anyone else since that first night when they'd bonded over two bottles of Prosecco, six gins, two large brandies, a chocolate buffet and a near-step-perfect dance to the 'Time Warp'. They picked the same excursions and made sure that whoever was up first saved their favourite beds at the pool—the ones near the bar but not too near the large family from Grimsby.

As they settled down, they perused the menu.

"I think I'm going to have the Beef Wellington," said Jane. Daisy turned her nose up, and Jane noticed. "Do you not like beef?"

"I don't eat any food that I can't see. Anything wrapped in pastry is a big no in my book. People who shop in Gregg's must be very trusting."

"I can't say I've ever been in a Gregg's. I'm not even sure if they have one in my town."

"You live in Hampshire, not on the Moon." Daisy rolled her eyes, but Jane didn't notice.

A waiter came over and took their order, returning soon after with a chilled bottle of Prosecco. The two women pounced on their wine the second he left the table.

They talked incessantly over their meal, and they laughed. They laughed a lot. Once the table was cleared and the wine bottle was emptied, they made their way to the Sunset Bar. They preferred it there to the Cabaret Lounge. The last time they were in there, they had been thrown a lot of disapproving looks when they shouted to the knife thrower's assistant, who was tied to a board, "It's a good job you're bandy!" after a knife had come precariously close to the assistant's right calf. After being told to keep it down, they decided to leave, declaring that the cabaret was "shit anyway."

The Sunset Bar, while more intimate, was noisier and attracted loud people, which suited Daisy and Jane better. Daisy found a table, and Jane went to the bar; she returned clutching a bottle of Prosecco in a silver chiller and two glasses. Once they were settled and in position, they began to scan the room.

"Gandalf has ventured out of Mordor, judging by the colour of his face," whispered Daisy out of the side of her mouth, drawing Jane's attention to an elderly gentleman with a long white beard and a very red face.

"Why do people go mad the last day of their holiday and feel the need to fry themselves to within an inch of their lives?" sniffed Jane. Daisy was reminded that her bra strap was digging into bright-pink flesh underneath her sequinned sleeve and decided not to comment.

"Still no sign of H4. Do you think Carl killed her by exhaustion?"

"No. I saw her today at the buffet, shouting to Andres to find some Hermesetas. He had no idea what she was talking about."

"It's a good job she didn't go in the pool today. After the lengthy session she had with Carl, we could have lost half the pool water if she'd jumped in. I'm surprised she can walk at all."

And so it began. A lengthy and enjoyable bitching session about all of the passengers who had sailed around the Caribbean with them for the last twelve days.

Before they knew it, it was midnight, and after they had both admitted to not having packed a thing for their departure the following day, they called it a night.

They were on different decks of the ship, but their cabins were the same. Daisy's was paid for from James' life insurance money, while Jane's trip had been funded by her generous divorce settlement. Daisy didn't know the details of the divorce, but from the brief conversation she'd had with Jane, she got the feeling the divorce was more Derek's idea than hers.

As they reached the lift to take them back to the decks, Daisy asked Jane to join her for a moment on a nearby sofa.

"Would you like to stay in touch?"

"Oh, I would." Jane seemed pleased.

"I'm not a big one on social media. I used to be on it, but our Cheryl caused some trouble a couple of years back, so I came off it. The less I know, the better I sleep. Now, I know writing letters is old-fashioned, but do you fancy keeping in touch by email?"

Jane was beaming and began to rummage in her sensible black leather bag for a pen. Daisy was confident that she would have one, and if pushed, the bag could probably reveal a sewing kit, various tablets for various ailments and a spare pair of stockings.

As predicted Jane produced an expensive-looking pen and a green notebook. She handed both to Daisy and asked her to write her email address on the blank page offered. Daisy took both and pulled the top off the pen to reveal a fountain nib. She studied it suspiciously. Jane noticed.

"It's a shame writing letters is a dying art, but I have a Mac now. I'm sure that will bring me just as much pleasure." Jane smiled.

"I wish I had a Mac," Daisy said. She couldn't be sure, but she got the impression Jane was bragging. "Or a John. Even a Tony would do me." She laughed, and when she was satisfied Jane's brag had landed back on her lap, Daisy began to scratch her email address into the notebook. "There. I haven't got any paper, so you just email me first, and I'll get yours then."

Jane agreed and put the pen and book back into her sensible bag. "Shall we say goodbye now?" She looked a little sad. They could meet in the morning and have breakfast, but Jane's coach to the airport was early for the flight to Gatwick, while Daisy's flight to Manchester was later in the day. Daisy simply nodded, and they both stood at the same time and scooped each other up.

In their twelve days, they had bonded, shared wine, shared the same sense of humour and revealed they were a little lonely since their husbands had gone. The relief they both felt when they admitted to their loneliness over a bottle of wine strengthened their fledgling friendship. Within a few days, they had divulged more of themselves to each other than they had to friends they had known for years.

"Thank you for making this holiday such an absolute pleasure," Jane whispered into Daisy's ear as they embraced. "You have no idea how much this has meant to me."

Daisy pulled back and looked at Jane. She could see the genuine emotion and affection in her honey-brown eyes.

"I think I do, love."

To: daisyduke71@gomail.com
From: jane-hubbard@skycorres.co.uk
Date: Tuesday, 21st April 17:03

Dear Daisy

I hope this email finds you well. We have been home a week, and I feel like I haven't been away. I've spent the last week catching up with friends. Some friends I lost in the divorce from Derek, but that's no loss, especially Andy and Mandy. They couldn't merely have you over to their house for a meal and some drinks. No, they insisted we played games, and a favourite of theirs was game shows.

Some of them were not too bad, to be fair. I remember once winning a rather fetching tote bag during a round of *Bullseye*, and I did find Christmas *Blind Date* not only revealing, but I could never look at Paul the same way when he was asked, "Who would be your ideal date and why?" and he said, "Dale Winton." It was a surprise to all of us but no one as much as his wife, Alice. So, there's no loss.

Cathy and her husband Nathan are a lovely couple. They're friends from when Julian was at school. Derek has never met them, though. I don't think he ever picked up Julian from school, not even when I put my back out pushing Derek's Triumph when he broke down outside B&Q. A man in his overalls came to help me, but it was too late by then. I've not been back to the branch, since the man in the overalls said a few choice words to Derek at the time. Anyway, Nathan is from Jamaica, but you wouldn't think so, as his roast dinners are the best I've ever tasted.

There's also my friend Julie. She works in a department store, but it's a decent one, so she has a fabulous collection of shoes and the latest range of Le Creuset.

I came home to lots of mail for Derek. I'm not entirely sure where he's living now. He tends to turn up out of the blue, which I find a bit rude. He keeps saying it's his house, and I have to remind him that he might have paid for it, but it's mine in name. I may go to his office and drop his mail off, but the last time I did that, he shouted me out of the building, calling me a spy. I only went as his subscription to *The Railway Magazine* was due and they'd written to tell him about it. I must say, since he's left, he can be very hotheaded. Anyway, this email was just to make sure you made it home safely.

Looking forward to hearing from you.

Jane

x

P.S. Why is your email address Daisy Duke? Is that your maiden name, as I recall your name being Burton on the ship?

To: jane-hubbard@skycorres.co.uk
From: daisyduke71@gomail.com
Date: Friday, 24th April 20:02

Dear Jane

I was so glad to see your email sitting in my inbox. My emails are usually about penis enlargement, which I don't want, finance for a BMW, which I want (the BMW, not the finance bit) and how to painlessly remove chin hair, which is a lie (the painless bit).

I came home to find our Cheryl had been living here for a few days, as she'd had a fight with Kelvin about him turning vegetarian. She said she can't afford to be buying Linda McCartney on her Universal Credit. He then, apparently, told her that if she got maintenance off the kids' dads, then they wouldn't have to scrimp—fat chance of her getting money out of them. John's still inside for setting fire to the local Department for Work and Pensions office when they refused his emergency loan application for a holiday to Ibiza. He kept telling them he could get work out there deejaying, but they turned him down flat.

He's learning to sew inside now and thinks he's going to be the next Giorgio Armani. He'd be lucky to sell socks in George at Asda. He still writes to our Bruno, who's ten. Then there's Steven, who upped and left as soon as she said she was pregnant with our Beyoncé, who's eight. He was last seen getting on a National Express bound for Brighton, wearing a pink trilby and a belt to match. The twins' (Sharpay and Troy) dad has never been revealed, so he's either married, dead or was sitting next to Steven on the National Express. The twins were six last month.

Kelvin's not a bad lad, to be fair. He had a job selling seafood around the pubs, but he reckons that went tits up when they banned smoking in pubs and they all started closing down. He's done a bit here and there, like Argos over Christmas, but they didn't keep him on. I think it's because he was caught riding the conveyor belt, but he says it was because he was overqualified and the boss knew it. I'm not so sure.

So our Cheryl has been here with all the kids, and boy, could I tell. Four days they were here, but you'd think they were here for four weeks. Not a bit of food left in the cupboard and a ring around the bath that a whole tub of Vim struggled with. I should take the key off her, but then I think it *is* her home, and our Beyoncé said it was lovely sleeping in my bed with her mam. She said the smell reminded her of the launderette on their estate. They do candles that smell of clean linen, so I'll pop one in her birthday box, and when she lights it, she can think of me (not in a religious way, though). Anyway, Cheryl's made up with Kelvin now, which is just as well as he's babysitting tomorrow while we go to Cheryl's mate Jade's birthday party. She asked me to go because I know Jade's mum from when they were at school. Nice lady, as I recall. We didn't keep in touch. Shame, as I thought she was quite down to earth even though she drove a car with beaded seat covers.

My flight back was delayed, which I wouldn't have minded only H4 moaned and moaned to anyone wearing a neck scarf and red lipstick. What does she want the trolley dollies to do? Magic a plane up from thin air? She sat there, constantly moving her arse on the chair like a dog with worms. So God knows what leaving present Carl has given her. When she shouted that no one was listening to her, I told her it was because the echo from between her legs was drowning her out. She tried to give me a dirty look, but it's like water off a duck's back when you've been on holiday in Cleethorpes with our Cheryl and forgotten to bring the Nintendo DS.

We were only delayed by three hours. I wasn't bothered at all. If James had been there, he'd have kicked up a stink. He would probably have asked for a seat next to H4, and then I'd be home running to the chemist and boiling his underwear. Not that my James was a ladies' man, but the man who sat next to her on the plane was trying to keep his distance from her with all her seat writhing and nearly got his head knocked off by the Duty-Free trolley.

Well, I'll go now. I'll let you know how the party goes. I'm looking forward to it and having a dance—I miss our dancing nights.

Love Daisy

P.S. My name is Daisy Duke because James said I had a look of General Lee. I didn't get the joke, but it amused him. My maiden name was Shane, and yes, I was glad to get rid of it.

XXX

To: **daisyduke71@gomail.com**
From: **jane-hubbard@skycorres.co.uk**
Date: **Wednesday, 29th April 08:15**

Dear Daisy

Thank you for clearing up my question about your name. Derek was a fan of *The Dukes of Hazzard* too.

I've had a quiet week. I managed to coordinate my wardrobe according to the season, but I admit I did struggle with anything made from polyester. What are your thoughts? I was also surprised at how much leisure wear I had. I've given a lot of it to the charity shop but kept most of the yoga wear. I try to do yoga every day now. I could only manage a couple of days a week when Derek was here. He said if the angels wanted us to sit in silence with legs like a pretzel, they wouldn't have invented the three-piece suite. In the end, I could only go when he was playing golf. I still try and go to the class a couple of times a week and do my own at home. Do you have a keep-fit regime? How do you keep your womanly figure? Derek was always watching what I ate. He said I should strive for the body of John Cleese. He likes his women lean, I suppose.

I'm going to take some time today to sort out Julian's room. He's not lived here since he married Carrie five years ago. She's a lovely girl and an excellent match for Julian. They met in the shop she works in. He went in to buy an air hammer, and when she suggested one with a quick-change chuck, it was love at first sight. Derek took some convincing that she was 'the one'. He said if the angels wanted women working in car accessory shops, then they wouldn't have invented the crossbar bicycle. He soon came around when she gave him a pair of spark-plug pliers for his birthday. They completely outshone the hair-and-nose clippers I gave him.

Julian and Carrie had a small wedding in Italy. They don't have many friends, so it made sense, I suppose. Carrie still works in the same shop, and Julian has been made manager of his team. Did I tell you he works for a centre that sells walking holidays for the obese? It's to promote healthier living, and I understand, from what he's told me, that his job is a real challenge. I mean, how can you tell from a cold call on the phone if someone is overweight? He says you have to win them around before you dive in with, *"Has anyone ever commented that you're too large to go on a roller coaster?"* or *"Would you deem a Fiat 500 too small for you to drive?"* I can see where he's coming from. You can't just ask if they're overweight, can you?

Anyway, as I said, I think it's time to sort out his room. I may turn it into a yoga studio. It will seem strange when I take down his posters of Carol Vorderman and Deborah Meaden, but I need to accept that it's just me now, and I should be happy that I can do with this house as I see fit.

I hope you have a lovely time at Jade's birthday party. Attach some pictures if you take any.

Jane

x

To: jane-hubbard@skycorres.co.uk
From: daisyduke71@gomail.com
Date: Friday, 8th May 10:14

Dear Jane

Thank you for your last email. It was so nice to hear a little more about your family. I remember you said you had a son when we were sunbathing that day and had to sit by the family from Grimsby. Do you remember the dad was covered in tattoos of his children? Well, we thought they must have been his children even though they looked like the cast of *The Goonies*. Still, that's love for you.

I went to Jade's party with our Cheryl. I've attached a couple of pictures for you. It's a good job we took these when we did. There was a huge fight about an hour after the one of me doing 'Oops Upside Your Head'. Jade's ex-boyfriend turned up, shouting the odds about why he wasn't invited. He then screamed all over the community centre that she aborted his baby before they split up. She was screaming at him, telling him that she'd only gone to help Mike on the meat wagon that day, and that's why she had blood on her grey leggings. She kept telling him that she wasn't pregnant, and if she had been, she wouldn't have had an abortion.

Anyway, to cut a long story short, Cheryl and I had to sort locking up the community centre, as Jade's brother said Jade had gone off in a taxi with the same ex-boyfriend. I told Cheryl I was surprised, but she said she could see it coming when the DJ played 'Don't Go Breaking My Heart' by Elton John and Kiki Dee. Apart from that, we had a wonderful night. I was even asked out on a date. His name is Dean. He's a bit older than me—well, I think he is, judging by his corduroy trousers. I gave him my number, but I've not heard from him. Not that I'm bothered.

I think I would feel strange going out with another man after James. I mean, it's all going Dutch now, and they all seem to have sex very quickly these days. He'll be whipping out a condom as soon as I've put my calculator away. Our Cheryl asked who he was; apparently, he is Jade's boss. He owns the local garden centre, and our Cheryl says he has a few bob and a big house in Didsbury. That's all she knows so far. She said she'd ask Jade more when she sees her, but no one has caught sight of her since the taxi ride. I told Cheryl she should check that her mate is okay, but she said Jade's fine, as Robby from the pizza place had delivered a gluten-free pizza to the ex-boyfriend's house, and it was a sixteen-inch. Jade hasn't been able to eat bread since she got caught short queuing for Take That tickets when they last toured. She polished off a twelve-inch Subway roll while she waited. She didn't make the concert or a toilet after a short digestion. Bless her.

In reply to your question in your email about polyester, I tend to try and split them all up in the wardrobe. I once put them all together, and the static generated from when I pulled my best cream blouse out nearly started a small fire. So that's my only tip regarding clothing. Except maybe buy all 'non-iron' clothes with a degree of scepticism.

I don't do yoga. Our Cheryl put me off, saying they're always breaking wind in the class. If I want to be in a room full of people breaking wind, I can make friends with a load of vegetarians and invite them over for a cup of green tea and eat cauliflower rice. Anyway, I get enough exercise running around my four grandkids. Cheryl keeps telling me to retire now I have her dad's pension. I know I'm fifty-nine, but I like working in the surgery. She only wants me to give up some of my hours so I can take the kids to street dance. I've told her that I'm not giving up my receptionist job so I can stand next to some competitive mum wearing a crop top called Mandy (the woman is called Mandy, not her top). She said there's no one there called Mandy, so I had no excuse.

I may look into something, though. There are classes in the community centre where Jade had her party. As you so eloquently put it, my womanly body is due to the menopause, so you must tell me how you kept your masculine frame.

Hope to hear from you soon.

Love Daisy

xxx

To: daisyduke71@gomail.com
From: jane-hubbard@skycorres.co.uk
Date: **Friday, 15th May 17:14**

Dear Daisy

I'm so glad the party was a success, even with the heated performance. I do hope by the time you read this that Jade's whereabouts have been confirmed. I was once locked in a toilet when I went shopping in Westfield in Stratford, and Derek didn't look for me for over two hours. He thought I might have gone to Laura Ashley to look at tie-backs. When I told him that it would be hard to be entertained by tie-backs for two hours, he said he had no idea what a tie-back did and how the hell would he know how long it took to look at them? I couldn't argue with that.

I think that was the last time we went shopping together. After that, he always insisted he go shopping on his own. He could fill a whole day at the shops and not come home with a thing. The only time I recall him ever buying anything was at Christmas and birthdays, and I suspect he had someone from his office help him with that. I once found a beautiful black kimono at the bottom of his wardrobe just before Christmas. When I didn't get it on Christmas Day, I asked him about it. He said he sent it back because it was so flimsy I might be tempted to put the heating up. The grey fleece one he bought me from Next was far more practical. He was sensible like that.

I've finished clearing Julian's room. It took me two days to dismantle his IKEA bed and wardrobe. It wouldn't have taken me that long if Derek hadn't glued every screw in when he built them. When I asked him why he had to use adhesive as well as screws, he said he refused to believe that Sweden was built with nothing more than an Allen key and an ABBA soundtrack.

I've decided the room will be my Zen space. I've started meditating, and I think I may become a Buddhist. But I will check and see if I have to shave my head first. I help organise the village fête each year, and I'm not sure the committee would accept such a bold statement. Would I still be able to help if I'm a Buddhist, as most, if not all who help and attend are Christian?

Until I find out, I'll just repaint the room and buy some plants, maybe a bonsai tree. I've bought *The Life-Changing Magic of Tidying Up: The Japanese Art of Decluttering and Organizing* by Marie Kondo. I actually purchased it last week, but now I can't find it.

I have to say, I was surprised that you think I have a masculine frame, but the beauty of having smaller breasts means they stay perkier for longer.

Anyway, I must go now. I've spent the whole day making a Persian stew and don't want it to spoil.

Jane

x

P.S. Thank you for the photographs of Jade's party. I didn't know you could get icing that colour. The penis was very realistic as well. Are the family Jewish?

To: jane-hubbard@skycorres.co.uk
From: daisyduke71@gomail.com
Date: **Sunday, 17th May 21:47**

Dear Jane

I've only just read your email now. I've been so busy the last few days. Dean from Didsbury called. Apparently, he didn't think it was right to call when I told him that I kiss my George every night before I go to bed. Jade cleared the matter up, telling him that I was a widow and the George I kiss is my George Clooney calendar hanging in the kitchen. He called, and we went out for a lovely meal last night not far from his garden centre. He picked me up in his Transit van, which I was a bit miffed at as I was wearing ten denier and my best olive-green dress. He said he doesn't have a regular car. I told him it must be a bugger to park in the supermarket, but he gets home delivery, so I guess that's that problem solved. But I did feel self-conscious in my dress getting out of a van with *Green & Moist* painted on the side.

The restaurant was very nice. You would have liked it, as there were a lot of things in sauces. I had a mushroom starter and a steak for main. I didn't get a pudding. A bit too early in the relationship to start eating Eton Mess in front of him. I tried to split the bill with him, but he wouldn't hear of it. Then, at the end of the night, he dropped me off and walked me to my front door. I didn't kiss him. I wanted to, but he had a rogue piece of broccoli stuck in his top teeth. I think he thought I was being coy, but if you remember from the night we had the flan, I don't like broccoli. He took my number, and we've been texting a fair bit. He likes using emojis a lot, and I have to ask our Beyoncé what they all mean. Why he can't just talk like a normal person is beyond me. I wonder if he is dyslexic, though. But I doubt it, as there are no spelling mistakes on the side of his van.

I had Cheryl, Kelvin and the kids over for Sunday lunch today. I do love it when they come over, but they make such a mess. Our Bruno knocked his cola all over my cream carpet, and then Kelvin tried to clean it with BLEACH! It's completely stripped the colour in a huge circle. Then our Cheryl said it was okay and covered it with an old mat she found in the garage. Now I have an armchair under the window with a doormat that reads 'I Can See Your Underwear'. James bought it from a lovely little novelty shop when we went on holiday in Cornwall. I put it in the garage when he died. Whenever I was going out or coming in, I was paranoid if I didn't have matching knickers and bra. Like the mat was going to tell people. So, I'll either have to buy a new rug or replace the carpet. I'll probably replace the carpet. Since the mat has been down, my paranoia has returned, and I've been living in my jeggings.

Anyway, they've left now with four bags of clean washing and the school uniforms all pressed. She used to go to the launderette on her estate but stopped when the owner complained that our Bruno was pushing crisp packets through the detergent drawer. You can't blame him in a way. He was trying to get them clean for an art project at school. He was trying to recreate The Last Supper and needed more beef flavoured Hula Hoop packets for Judas's hair. Since then, she's not been allowed in there, and the next nearest one is past my house, so she might as well come here.

I do all her washing, and she pays me by doing all of her ironing, except for the school uniforms, which I do, and anything frilly. Oh, and pleats. She can't do pleats.

Well, I'm pooped, so I'll say good night. Let me know if you've finished your Zen room. I toyed with the idea of having one, but all that deep breathing makes me dizzy.

Love

Daisy

xxx

To: daisyduke71@gomail.com
From: jane-hubbard@skycorres.co.uk
Date: Tuesday, 26th May 14:55

Dear Daisy

I was excited to read your email about your date with Dean. He sounds like a true gentleman. You must send me a picture of him. What happened to his first wife? Does he have any children? And how did he have his steak in the restaurant? I think you can tell a lot from a man by how he has his steak. Derek always liked his steak very well done. He said if the angels wanted us to have our steak rare, they wouldn't have invented British Gas.

I've finished my Zen room. I've attached some photographs. Please be honest and tell me what you think. I've been meditating in there most days and find just sitting in the silence very soothing. Then when I've finished in there, I sometimes take a run into town. Do you know I can walk around all day and not see Derek, even though his office is practically on the street that I'm walking on? He must be terribly busy with work.

I'm sure I told you he's still running the business I helped start and build. In the beginning, it was just him and me. We had one phone (in the back bedroom that doubled as an office) and a lot of enthusiasm. But with Julian being born and then Derek wanting me home, I left the business. By then, we had premises, staff, and many clients I had brought in. The business was booming, and as far as I can tell, it still is. I do miss it sometimes. The hours could be long, and by the time I asked Derek to leave, he was always in the office or working away. So I hardly noticed him gone at all when he did go.

I was hoping to bump into him, as I had his hair and nose clippers in my tote bag. I'm sure he must need them by now. Before I bought them, his nose and ears reminded me of the local car wash. I would have gone in, but after the scene he caused last time, I thought it best just to hope I bumped into him. Maybe he's not going out because of the abundance of hair now growing from various orifices. Do you think I should just go in? It's funny, none of the staff know who I am. They've all been replaced.

Your email about Cheryl gave me the idea of inviting Julian and Carrie over for Sunday lunch. They said they have some news for me. I'm hoping that Carrie's shop has the car seat leather cleaner back in stock. My Mercedes is not looking its best. I went to the bakery the other day and left a cashmere cardigan casually draped over the seat to cover the neglect. Do you have that trouble with your upholstery? You must tell me what you use. I would imagine a woman like you has lots of tips for removing dirt and grime. I'm disadvantaged in that area with having a cleaner for years. I had to let Lorna go after the divorce.

It wasn't the money, I hasten to add. No, it just seemed silly to keep her on when there was only me left in the house, and Lorna was so upset when I let her go. She said I was the easiest job on her round and the only person in the road with a Dyson vacuum cleaner. I'm very surprised Elizabeth

Sharples, at number fourteen, doesn't have one. She was the first in the street to have a George Foreman grill.

I'll go now and plan my menu for when Julian and Carrie come over. I hope Carrie likes couscous. I watched Nigella do a rather splendid recipe the other night involving daikons. The ingredient will look delightful against my best Royal Doulton. Do you like daikons?

Jane

x

To: jane-hubbard@skycorres.co.uk
From: daisyduke71@gomail.com
Date: Saturday, 30th May 10:15

Dear Jane

Just thought I would send a quick email before I go to the hairdresser's. I have a date tonight with Dean from Didsbury. We're going out for a meal with some of his friends. I'm a bit nervous to tell you the truth. I've bought a new dress from John Lewis, and our Cheryl is lending me her floral open-toed shoes. There will be two other couples joining us. One of the couples is celebrating a wedding anniversary. Dean said he met them years ago when he started a gardening course at the local poly.

Thanks for attaching the photographs of your Zen room. It looks very nice. With not knowing what Zen is exactly, is it normal not to have any furniture at all? The bonsai tree looked very lonely in the corner on the floor, but I'm sure you know best.

In reply to your upholstery question, my car, a Toyota Picnic, does not have leather seats. Though they would be so much easier to clean after the grandkids have been in there. Sharpay and Troy have still not learned to tell me they want the toilet when they first feel it. They only tell me when they're mid-flow or worse. I blame all these Tena Lady adverts. It gives the kids the wrong impression. But I'm sure if I were driving around in a Mercedes, I'd wrap the kids in cling film before they could climb in.

As for cleaning tips, I find good old-fashioned soap and water cleans most things. I never had a cleaner and never ever thought of having one. There was only our Cheryl, and she wasn't a bad kid. The messy years came when she started using fake tan. Her bedroom looked like she had a paintball match in there and Rimmel made the bullets, and all of my good towels were like the Turin Shroud. I'm not sure I would have liked a cleaner going through all my stuff. I think a person's dirt is their responsibility.

Anyway, I must go; otherwise, I'll be late. Let me know how it goes with Julian and Carrie when they come over for lunch tomorrow. I'm sure your couscous and Daleks will be a hit.

Love

Daisy

xxx

To: daisyduke71@gomail.com
From: jane-hubbard@skycorres.co.uk
Date: **Sunday, 31st May 21:03**

Dear Daisy

I have some exciting news. Julian and Carrie have just left after a wonderful afternoon, and you're the first person I'm sharing this with. Carrie is pregnant. I'm absolutely delighted. I wasn't sure if Julian could impregnate her, as he rode his bicycle to school for years and the saddle was particularly invasive. But it seems that all is well, and there you go. I will be a grandmother sometime at the beginning of December. I tried to call Derek and tell him the news while Julian was here, but he didn't pick up. I texted him to say I'd called and there must be something wrong with his phone as the ringtone sounded strange, foreign even. He texted back to say he couldn't get to the phone and I should text him with whatever I needed to say. Julian said he would call him later tonight when he knew his father was back, and when I asked where he was, he replied that he'd just gone to the shops. How Julian knew that, I don't know.

My Zen room is supposed to be clear. I may put a small table in there for the bonsai tree, as it's leaving a dent in the carpet. Nothing that requires a doormat, though. Julian was unhappy when he saw what I'd done to his room. I explained that he never stayed in the house anymore, and if he ever did, there was still a spare bedroom for him and Carrie. I also packed all of his belongings very carefully. I've gone through twenty metres of bubble wrap on his ventriloquist dummies alone. (A hobby he had in his mid-teens for a couple of years.) Derek once said that he was sick of him talking out of the side of his mouth, so he thought he should turn it into something worthwhile. However, a nasty fight between Julian and a boy called Gary put an end to his ventriloquism when Julian hit the boy for calling his prized dummy, Lily Dew, a rude word saying it sounded like something else. To this day, I'm still unsure what the boy was referring to. Carrie said she would not have them in their house, as Lily Dew and, in particular, Thin Lizzy give her the creeps. She actually went as far as to say that Lizzy reminded her of Ken Barlow. So, they're still all boxed and in my garage. I'm not sure if they'll ever make it to Julian's house. Maybe once the baby is born, she might relent and see that they could be used as playthings for the baby at a later date.

I'm now wondering whether to turn the Zen room into a nursery. I do have a couple of spare rooms. One is set up for guests already, and the other houses boxes full of Derek's railway magazines, Haynes manuals and old bills. I may use that room instead. I'm just unsure how Derek will react if I say I've moved his stuff. What do you think I should do?

I hope you have had a lovely time with Dean.

Jane

x

To: daisyduke71@gomail.com
From: jane-hubbard@skycorres.co.uk
Date: Wednesday, 10th June 19:14

Dear Daisy

I hope all is well. It's been a while since your last email. I'm sure you've just been busy with your grandchildren and your job and busy social life.

Jane

x

To: daisyduke71@gomail.com
From: jane-hubbard@skycorres.co.uk
Date: Friday, 12th June 18:18

Dear Daisy

Are you alive? If so, please reply. If not, who shall I contact?

Jane

x

To: jane-hubbard@skycorres.co.uk
From: daisyduke71@gomail.com
Date: Saturday, 13th June 16:01

Dear Jane

You will be pleased to know I'm alive and well and back home. I've been back home a week but just haven't had a chance to write to you. Sorry for making you worried. I was at Dean's house in Didsbury. He has a lovely home. Six bedrooms, four bathrooms and a room he uses just for cleaning his guns. He's not an assassin or anything like that. He likes to go shooting for game. I can't say I approve, and I daren't tell Kelvin. He's still being vegetarian. However, he still eats burgers, sausages, bacon, and chops. When I asked him what he doesn't eat, he said fish. When I said I didn't know he liked fish, he said he didn't, and that's why it was easy for him to become a vegetarian.

I stayed at Dean's the night of the meal with his friends. They're very nice. Richard and his wife Nicola were celebrating eleven years of marriage. Lovely couple they were. Richard is a landscape gardener, and his wife sells cakes online for home delivery. I didn't know you could do that. My letterbox is quite high, though, and I would imagine that a drop like that could have a detrimental effect on any decorative feature. I can bake myself anyway, so I doubt I'll ever feel the need to buy her Bedfordshire Clanger.

The other couple, Jacob and Lauren, were lovely too. Jacob has a small herb farm and distributes to local businesses.

Lauren helps him with his admin and organises distribution. They live out Rivington way, not that far.

So, at the end of the night, we got a taxi, and I wasn't taking any notice which direction we were going. Next thing, we were pulling up outside Dean's house, and he was inviting me in for coffee. Well, I stayed for six days! And no, I was not in the spare bedroom. I told work I was sick. I'm never off sick, so I figured it was about time. I tried to come home after three days when I said I couldn't keep wearing his clothes, but he wouldn't hear of it. I think he's quite besotted, or he has a sex addiction. I don't mind which one, to be honest. If Carl was pulling moves with H4 like Dean was with me, it's no wonder she was walking sideways.

I always thought James and I had a good sex life, but looking back, I suppose it became quite stale. Don't get me wrong, I enjoyed it with him, but I've never had sex and thought I might need to take a break halfway through. Dean has the body of a man half his age. James was always a little podgy, but we both liked our food, and I liked feeding him. I did feel a little self-conscious when Dean first took my dress off, as I had my large pull-ins on. I thought he might struggle to get them off due to high Lycra content, but he's ripped, and so were the pants, eventually.

Our Cheryl was worried sick about me, especially when Jade told her that Dean had not been in the garden centre for a few days. She went to the house, and once she realised I wasn't lying dead on the floor, she left with the eight pints of milk stacked up on the doorstep. I texted her to say I was with a friend, but I think she knew who I was with.

By last night, I realised I had to come home. I've lost nine pounds and a fair amount of self-consciousness in a week. Plus, the grandkids were texting me, asking me when I could take them pony riding. I said not for a few weeks yet. I don't think my undercarriage could bear it.

I've attached a photo of me and Dean. It was taken when we had the meal in the restaurant. The meal was lovely, and we both had the fish, so I'm not sure what Derek would deduce from that if he only judges steak eaters.

May I finally say congratulations. Your news about you becoming a grandmother must be very welcome. If Julian and Carrie are anything like our Cheryl, you'll be rushed off your feet. I've never had a minute or a full cupboard since they were born. Will they find out the sex before it is born? Our Cheryl had surprises with all of hers. She didn't want to know.

Regarding your spare rooms, you should do what you damn well like and blow Derek! Throw all of his stuff out and turn it into the nursery. I would have liked a nursery in this house, but our Cheryl fired them out like a Tommy Gun, so the spare room looks more like a hostel, to be honest. Sorry if I worried you by not replying straight away.

Lots of love

Daisy

xxx

To: daisyduke71@gomail.com

From: jane-hubbard@skycorres.co.uk

Date: Friday, 19th June 11:11

Dear Daisy

I was so pleased to get your email and a little relieved. I was also surprised that you went to Dean's for six days. His coffee must be amazing. Lol.

I take it you got over your nerves having sex with someone else. I have only ever been with Derek. He made me smile on occasion, so I guess his performance would be rated as adequate. Compared to some of the scenes I see on television, I would also add 'limited' to his repertoire. But then again, maybe it was me. Maybe I was the boring one. I guess I'll never know now. It was the same every time, a quick fumble up top, then bottom, climb on, climb off, and then I would make him a cup of tea with two Hob Nobs on the side.

I asked Julian how his father took the news about him becoming a grandfather, and he said he was pleased. When I asked for more information, he became very guarded. I don't know why. It's not like what the man says or does has any effect on me. They also said they would find out the sex of the baby. I have to agree with them. I wanted to know when I was carrying Julian. I think when you find out, it helps you prepare. I knew all of the names of the characters of *Button Moon* and *Fraggle Rock* and became acquainted with the rules of *Crackerjack* before he was born. I felt it gave me a head start. However, when he was a toddler, he only liked to play with his 'thing' and the knobs on my Zanussi washing machine.

I've decided I will contact Derek and ask him to collect the remainder of his belongings in the spare room, then I'll convert that into the nursery. I've found a lovely set in Mothercare if it's a boy, which I have a feeling it is, as she said she's already craving chocolate and fancies Richard Madeley. I was exactly the same. I'm still not sure where Derek is living, so I'll have to text him or find out from Julian. I don't know why he's so secretive about it. I do wonder if he's living in a bedsit and feels ashamed. Part of me hopes he is, but then he is the father of my child and the grandfather of my future grandchild, so I really should be a little kinder and hope he's sunk no lower than a maisonette.

Thank you for attaching a picture of you and Dean. He looks very nice, like a young Declan Donnelly, only older. Has anyone ever said that to him before? Is he short? It's hard to tell from your photograph. I will admit I like tall men. But then, I am a statuesque five-foot-ten.

I do like that dress you're wearing. Not many people would have the confidence to wear horizontal stripes with your body shape, yet you seem to carry it off without a care in the world. I do admire your boldness.

I shall go now. I want to catch the florist before he runs out of peonies. I want Derek to see that standards have not slipped if he comes over and collects his things.

Jane

x

To: jane-hubbard@skycorres.co.uk
From: daisyduke71@gomail.com
Date: Monday, 22nd June 23:42

Dear Jane

I thought I would have an early night, but I couldn't sleep. I guess all those late nights with Dean from Didsbury have buggered up my body clock. I find myself staring at the ceiling, worrying about our Cheryl and the kids, and then I start worrying about work. My job isn't exactly taxing, though. All I have to do is answer the phone, make appointments, do a bit of filing, and take an awful lot of abuse from the patients. I had one gentleman last month who had that many ailments I cracked a joke saying he needed a priest, not a doctor. Well, that was it! He thought that gave him the green light to get on his soapbox about me being presumptuous about him being a Christian. I told him straight that the only thing I could presume with certainty was his symptoms were linked to gonorrhoea, and if he continued with that tone, I would make sure the rest of the surgery could comment on my presumption. They soon sit down once they know I won't take any of their nonsense.

Anyway, I only saw Dean on Friday night. He came over, and I cooked him a meal. I'd been cooking and baking all day, and he was very complimentary about my soft buns. He didn't stay the night. He had an early delivery arriving at his garden centre. We said we'd catch up during the week, which suits me fine. I don't want to see him too often; otherwise, I'll be walking down both sides of the street at the same time at this rate.

Thank you for your comments about my stripy dress. Dean said I looked stunning in it. I'm not sure what you mean about my body shape. I can only presume you mean my ample chest. I'm sure someone of your angular proportions could also look just as good.

Now, about Derek: I really think you should investigate more as to his whereabouts. I'm sure he's not living in a bedsit. Do they even have them in Hampshire? I would go around to the office and ask him straight. He knows where you live, so why shouldn't you know where he lives? What's the big secret? I would've thought he'd want to speak to you about the baby, at the very least.

I cannot believe that Carrie is having cravings already. I craved vindaloo curry and milk of magnesia in my last two months. I think that's why James had the en suite installed while I was carrying her. Since then, we always had separate bathrooms, and to this day, I still don't use his. It still smells of his Lynx and CK One aftershave. Sometimes I go in there just to smell him. I think our Cheryl does as well, but she'd never tell me.

Well, I must try and get some sleep now. Let me know how things go with Derek.

Love Daisy

xxx

To: daisyduke71@gomail.com
From: jane-hubbard@skycorres.co.uk
Date: Thursday, 25th June 15:23

Dear Daisy

I have awful news. I don't even know where to start. I took your advice and played detective about where Derek was living. I asked him straight, and he wouldn't tell me. He said I could just communicate with him via text, and anything that needed forwarding could be done via his office. So I decided to follow him. I knew he'd recognise the Mercedes straight away, so I asked my friends Cathy and Nathan if they'd help me. You remember Nathan, her Jamaican husband. Anyway, he said he would love to help. So, yesterday, Nathan and I did a kind of stakeout outside his office. We watched him get into the car with Olivia, his executive assistant, and then he went off in the direction of Lyndhurst.

Nathan and I figured he was dropping Olivia off, but then he pulled up to a rather large house. Nineteenth century, I would say, complete with stables and enough land to host the Grand National. Nathan and I got out of the car and hid in the rhododendrons at the end of the drive. That's then that I saw it. He opened the garage door to put his car away, and there was his old Triumph TR3. The same car that he said he'd sold more than five years ago when I insisted he sell it as I needed a new kitchen. Well, I didn't get the kitchen, and now I know why. He fobbed me off with an excuse about retirement and being able to enjoy cooking more when we had more time on our hands. He said he'd put the money into an ISA to gain interest until then. Nathan and I then watched (still from the bushes) him walk into the house after Olivia.

Daisy, I'm beginning to think he lives there. Nathan said we should go to the door and confront him, but I said no. What am I supposed to say? I'm not his wife anymore, and how do I explain I was following him with my Jamaican friend? If he saw us emerging from the shrubbery, he might think something is going on with Nathan and me. So it was either good sense or cowardice that made me retreat. My head is all in a spin about it. We haven't been divorced two years yet. How long has he been seeing her? Don't you think he's moved on a little quickly, even if it is to Lyndhurst? Do you think Julian knows anything? Should I ask him?

Please let me know what you think I should do.

Jane

x

To: jane-hubbard@skycorres.co.uk
From: daisyduke71@gomail.com
Date: Friday, 26th June 09:47

Dear Jane

I was so upset reading your email from last night. The only good thing about it was the fact you were not alone. My advice would be to ask Carrie. Julian may have spoken to her, and she may be more willing to tell you things, woman to woman like. Speaking to Julian directly might make him feel that he has to choose between his parents. I remember once asking Cheryl if she wanted to watch *Hannah Montana* with me or *Sabrina the Teenage Witch* with her father. The fallout lasted for days and resulted in Cheryl having Sky Multiroom installed in her bedroom—an expensive mistake once you add it up over the year.

If there's no joy there, then just talk to Derek direct. Tell him you had no choice but to follow him, as he won't tell you anything. Tell him he might have split from you, but he hasn't split from the family, and you're all a part of that—stand firm with him, Jane. You have done nothing wrong. Can I suggest when you do confront him, dress up a little? Let him see what he's missing.

Lots of love

Daisy

xxx

To: daisyduke71@gomail.com
From: jane-hubbard@skycorres.co.uk
Date: Tuesday, 30th June 19:11

Dear Daisy

I must have read your email a dozen times during the course of Friday. I decided to follow your advice and confront Derek, but I needed a little Dutch courage. So I drank a bottle of Remy Martin and passed out by five in the afternoon. It took me all weekend to get over the hangover, so I didn't go until today, as I was at the beautician's yesterday.

I did as you suggested and went to the office in all of my finery. I wore a dress from Reiss that I bought for a black-tie function Derek took me to a couple of years back. I paired that with my Louboutin shoes and my faux fur coat. I walked straight into his office and found him laughing with Olivia. He looked very shocked and said how dare I come unannounced and asked why I looked like Shirley Bassey wearing a fur coat in June. I told him it was always chilly whenever I was around him, especially in Lyndhurst. He went white, which was an achievement, seeing as he had a healthy tan. Olivia had one too, I noticed. I asked if they had a sunbed room in that big house in the country. Olivia began telling me they'd just returned from the Cayman Islands. I felt sick, and the coat wasn't helping. Derek then said that the office was not the place to have a deeply personal conversation and I was to meet him at the house in Lyndhurst.

Well, I went, and it's not Olivia's house. It's his and Olivia's AND their son's. Ben is seven years old. Derek's known Olivia for nine. I am in total shock. They even have a nanny named Lena, a skinny and insipid-looking woman from Warsaw. She walked in with the child, took one look at me and shooed the boy upstairs. Olivia ran after them both, and I never saw them again.

So they couldn't hear anything, Derek ushered me into a kitchen that looked like it was straight out of a magazine. Everything was surgically clean, and when he asked me what I wanted, I nearly said, "A facelift." Well, Derek went to start on me, but I stood my ground and steeled myself like I did the day before when I had my lip waxed. I told him to knock off the high-and-mighty act or I'd tell Olivia about the time when he 'disappeared' in Bangkok. He said if the angels wanted men to wear make-up, then why did they put the men's department so far away from the beauty department in Debenhams? He added that he'd appreciate it if I kept that story to myself. I can't divulge the details, Daisy, but let's just say he's never been able to look at a coconut without developing a twitch in his left leg.

So, I've found out that Derek has been leading a double life for nine years. He bought the house with her eight years ago, and not long after, she found out she was pregnant with Ben. I asked why he didn't leave me all those years ago, but he said he felt sorry for me. I have no idea why, as I've been perfectly fine without him, and when I told him so, he asked if staking him out in the high street in a Daewoo Matiz with a black man was classed as fine. I'd forgotten he knew what car Nathan drove. I told him he'd made a fool of me for years, and all I got was the house. I didn't push for any of the business even though I built it with him, thinking that was all he had.

And there was me thinking he was living in a bedsit, and all the time, he was living it up with his new family and driving around Lyndhurst with the child and his nanny in the back seat while Olivia probably gives them a rendition of 'We Are Family' by Sister Sledge.

I can't understand it, Daisy. Olivia is not his type at all. She's clearly too young for him (fifteen years, maybe more), she has at least a 38DD chest, and her bottom half is very curvy. Derek always liked his women to be incredibly slim. She has to be at least a size fourteen. Maybe she was a lot thinner when he met her, and when she was pregnant, she had an unfortunate craving. My friend craved Jaffa Cakes throughout her pregnancy with her second child, and now she can't even look at one or even a Terry's Chocolate Orange without feeling her bra tightening.

I asked him if we should tell Julian, but he said no. He said Julian knows he has another woman, but that's all, and Julian thinks he's only started seeing her recently. So Julian doesn't even know he has a half-brother. He covered the last nine years of our lives over a cup of Darjeeling tea and then walked me to the car. I tried to call Julian, but Carrie said he was at a meeting with the amateur dramatics. I then called my friend Julie, but her phone was turned off. That means she'll be doing promotions in the store. Cathy and Nathan go to a quiz night on a Tuesday, which left me with Mr Jacobs Creek and my Mac laptop, and here I am. Oh, Daisy, what am I to do? Who am I? Who is Derek? I do not know my husband anymore.

Jane

x

Dear Jane

Oh, my dear friend. What you must be going through! What an absolute arsehole. Who is Derek, indeed? He's a little shit, and he's not your husband anymore. He's your ex, which makes him someone else's problem. All those years of cooking, cleaning, raising his son and the embarrassment of Bangkok to find out he lives in Lyndhurst with his secretary. It's like one of those stories I read in my *Bella* magazine. I wish you lived nearer. I would've loved to have gone on a stakeout, and Derek wouldn't know my Toyota Picnic.

Why don't you come and stay here for a few days? Throw your toothbrush in your handbag and come to Chorley. You need to get away and have time to think. You can recharge your batteries, and we can go shopping in the Trafford Centre. I'll tell our Cheryl to keep away with the kiddies. She'll have to see if Jade can run the kids to trampolining. Mind you, they could knock it off for a week or two. Our Sharpay's eyes take a while to settle after a session, and she looks like a chameleon until the Sunday.

Say you'll come. I have new bedding from Dunelm, and I know you'll love it.

Lots of love

Daisy

xx

P.S. I'm not taking no for an answer.

P.P.S. I'll look after you xx

To: daisyduke71@gomail.com
From: jane-hubbard@skycorres.co.uk
Date: Wednesday, 1st July 18:02

Dear Daisy

Thanks for replying so quickly. You really are a true friend. If you don't mind, I think I will take you up on your offer. I'll drive down tomorrow and stay until Sunday if that's okay. By then, I'm sure you'll be fed up with me.

Jane

x

To: daisyduke71@gomail.com
From: jane-hubbard@skycorres.co.uk
Date: Monday, 6th July 07:15

Daisy

I would be very grateful if you could return my pillow that I left at yours at the weekend. I shall expect it by the end of the week.

Jane

To: jane-hubbard@skycorres.co.uk
From: daisyduke71@gmail.com
Date: Tuesday, 7th July 10:17

Jane

If you want your pillow, you know where it is. It'll stay there until tomorrow. If it's still on my spare bed by the end of the day, it will be making its way to the wheelie bin outside, which you felt was an eyesore and very 'Northern'.

Daisy

P.S. I hope the badgers have a field day with your flimsy bin bags.

To: daisyduke71@gomail.com
From: jane-hubbard@skycorres.co.uk
Date: Tuesday, 7th July 15:55

Daisy

Don't you dare throw away that pillow! It is a Dunlopillo. In fact, it's a Serenity Deluxe, so it probably costs more than the mattress it's sitting on.

Jane

To: jane-hubbard@skycorres.co.uk
From: daisyduke71@gomail.com
Date: Wednesday, 8th July 12:18

Jane

If you want your Dunnypillow, it's making its way to the landfill in Whittle-le-Woods. And I'll have you know that the mattress is quite happy without the extra addition of your pillow that was the weight of a breeze block. You probably left it because you didn't have the energy to lift it after the efforts you made chasing Dean all weekend. I'm sure he would pass on his best wishes if he wasn't still running for the hills after you tried to grab his bollocks under the table while I served toad-in-the-hole. You were told the bins would be collected.

Daisy

To: daisyduke71@gomail.com
From: jane-hubbard@skycorres.co.uk
Date: Wednesday, 8th July 12:40

Daisy

I was not going to make the five-hundred-mile trip for a pillow, and I did not grab his bollocks. I spilt wine on his trousers and was trying to help him clean himself.

Jane

To: jane-hubbard@skycorres.co.uk
From: daisyduke71@gomail.com
Date: Wednesday, 8th July 16:01

Jane

It's your pillow or was, and because of that, I was not prepared to make the ten-minute round trip to the Post Office. And Dean is not a child. He can clean his own bollocks after someone accidentally on purpose throws a glass of wine in his lap. And was it an accident when you called for him to fetch you a towel while you were in the shower? Yes, I heard about that. And I also heard about you timing your nightly wees with his. No doubt, you were standing there in your best John Lewis nightie. I've said all I have to say on the matter. Your pillow is dead, and so is this friendship.

Daisy

To: daisyduke71@gomail.com
From: jane-hubbard@skycorres.co.uk
Date: Friday, 10th July 23:21

Daisy

I have bought myself another pillow. Let's just forget about it.

Jane

To: daisyduke71@gomail.com

From: jane-hubbard@skycorres.co.uk

Date: Friday, 17th July 10:42

Daisy

I hope you're okay. I know a lot of things were said in anger, so let's just put it all behind us.

Jane

x

To: daisyduke71@gomail.com
From: jane-hubbard@skycorres.co.uk
Date: Saturday, 25th July 23:58

Dear Daisy

It's clear you're ignoring me. Please email me back. I did try to call you last week, but I think you may have blocked my number.

I'm sorry.

Jane

x

To: daisyduke71@gomail.com
From: jane-hubbard@skycorres.co.uk
Date: Tuesday, 4th August 20:12

Dear Daisy

I am so sorry for what I did. I'm a wicked person; I know that. I just wanted a man to find me attractive, and I did it all the wrong way. I told my friend Julie, the one who works in the department store, all about my weekend and my behaviour. While she applied my sea salt and mud mask, she told me in no uncertain terms that she would have thrown me out on the Friday when I shouted for the towel.

I admitted to her that I did time my shower while you went to Tesco to buy my favourite bottle of fizz and Dean was downstairs greasing your baking tins. The thing is, Daisy, I don't even find your Dean attractive. Oh, he's an attractive man, but not my type. I'm not sure what my type is, to be honest. I thought it was Derek, but the Derek I know now is not my type, either. He was my first real boyfriend. While everyone was discovering their sexuality to Adam & The Ants and Bucks Fizz, I was busy studying in a bedsit in Reading. I met Derek not long after I left uni, and the rest, as they say, is history.

I'll admit the whole Derek and Olivia thing has knocked me senseless. I'm drinking far too much, and I know Mrs Malone from next door was judging me when I filled the boot the other day with empty Prosecco bottles. I just cannot think straight. I find myself staring out of windows and wondering where did it all go wrong? Why did he leave me? Why didn't he leave me years ago when he first started the affair? It's clear he's in love with her. That day when I walked into the office and saw them laughing made me more sad than angry. Sad that I had never made him smile like that. I never noticed how white his teeth were until that day. Thinking about it, though, that could have been the tan.

Nevertheless, he looked marvellous, and she clearly is good for him. But what was it about me that made him look elsewhere? Was it the fact that I wasn't particularly adventurous? He wanted me to dress up years ago in the bedroom, and I refused. I thought it was odd, but now, looking back, I was simply frigid. There, I've said it! I'm too self-conscious. Well, I am when I'm sober. I drank far too much in your home, and I'm sorry that was how I behaved. I guess I just started thinking about how boring I was, and I thought to get over that was to jump on the first man I saw, and unfortunately, that happened to be Dean. Please tell him I am dreadfully sorry, and I will be happy to pay for his dry-cleaning bill for his pants.

But what I do want to fix is our friendship. While I have friends that I can see whenever I wish, I've never been able to talk to them like I can talk to you. I don't know if it's because my friends are not real friends or that it may be easier to talk to you via a computer, or the fact you come from Chorley. All I do know is in a short space of time, you have become one of the best friends I've ever had. You were the first person to challenge me about wearing tights in ninety-degree heat. You were the first person to tell me that it's okay to be the last in the bar, and you were the first person I told when Derek crushed what was left of my little world. So, please, Daisy. Please, please, please email me. I'll do anything to make it right.

Love

Jane xx

To: jane-hubbard@skycorres.co.uk
From: daisyduke71@gomail.com
Date: Wednesday, 12th August 07:14

Dear Jane

Thank you for your email and your eventual apology. I will admit I was very, very cross with you and your behaviour while you were here. But after reading your heartfelt words, I realise that some of your actions were a reaction to all that has happened to you. They say you take things out on the people you care about. So by my reckoning, after the way you carried on, you care about me a lot.

Let's draw a line underneath it all. I have passed your apology on to Dean. He accepted it gracefully and waived the offer of paying for his dry-cleaning. He said we would go shopping for new trousers the next time we go to Manchester.

Now, seeing as we're trying to get back on an even keel, how are things going? Have you heard from Derek? What has Julian said all about it? How is Carrie getting on with the pregnancy?

Lots of love

Daisy

xxx

To: daisyduke71@gomail.com
From: jane-hubbard@skycorres.co.uk
Date: Friday, 14th August 10:22

Dear Daisy

You have no idea how happy I was to see your email. Thank you for forgiving me. I promise I will never behave like that again. I also promise never to drink Bacardi again. It clearly doesn't agree with me, and although I'm not making excuses, I cannot recall a time when I've talked about David Attenborough with such sexual undertones.

In answer to your questions, I have not seen Derek but have spoken to him a couple of times on the phone. During the first call, he said that Olivia was upset about how things had developed during our last meeting. I told him to take her and their son back to the Caribbean; I was sure she would get over it then while I would happily continue with my life even though I found out my husband was having an affair for years, had fathered a child in secret, bought another house, never sold the TR3, and I still had not had the kitchen replaced. He went to argue with me, but I offered to go to Lyndhurst to show Olivia how to 'get a grip'. He told me there was no need for that, and this wasn't an episode of *Blind Date*. He clearly loves having women fight over him. Shame the idiot doesn't realise I threw the towel in the day the ink was dry on the decree absolute.

On the other hand, Julian was quite haughty when I told him that I knew his father was with Olivia. He then, and I don't mind saying, said he'd known for years even though his father didn't know this and bragged about his father having exotic holidays and living in Lyndhurst. When I asked him whether he had ever been, he said no. He said his father told him he and Carrie could go and visit once they were all settled in. I pointed out they'd been living there for eight years. Even the Pilgrim Fathers didn't take that long to settle, and they had moved across the world, not just off the A31.

I asked him if he wondered if he would have his own room when he stayed or if he would be expected to share with his little brother. That soon knocked his condescending tone on its arse. He blew his fuse about not being told about Ben and said he was going to his father's house immediately. He walked out, nearly tripping over his bottom lip. I didn't hear anything and called him a few days later. It took him a while to come to the phone. According to Carrie, he's in a deep depression over it all and was disappointed that the GP wouldn't make a house call to not only diagnose his depression but to refer him to a psychiatrist.

When he came to the phone, I asked him how it went with his father. He said he'd not seen him, as it dawned on him, after he'd stormed out of my home, that he didn't know the address. I offered to take him there when he was feeling up to it, but he declined the offer saying he would contact his father when he was more mentally stable. That could be a while, Daisy. He took to his bed for a week when Thatcher died.

So, until Julian musters up enough bottle to confront his dad, I will be in the dark as to how that will develop.

Carrie has not been much help with it all. But then again, she does have the pregnancy to worry about. She decided not to find out what sex the baby was and said she wanted it to be a surprise. Julian wasn't happy, and neither was I, to be honest. I'm not sure what colour clothes to buy, and they say you can confuse a child as soon as it's born. What if the child interprets Jemima Puddleduck as too feminine or Peter Rabbit too masculine? These decisions can have a profound effect on the child as it grows up, and although there is no evidence to back it up, you simply don't know if this has any bearing on confusing them about their sexual orientation. Don't get me wrong. I don't mind having a gay grandchild; on the contrary, they seem very avant-garde at the moment. I just worry that the poor child will not know whether to pin up posters of Beyoncé Knowles or Nick Knowles.

Well, I will sign off now. I'm baking cakes for the church village fête, which takes place tomorrow on the green. I could do without it, but the vicar said a fête without my caramel-nipped buns was a day he never wanted to witness.

Love

Jane

x

P.S. Just to reinforce my apology and also to illustrate that I am not a total basket case, I would love it if you could come to my little home in Hampshire. There are a few places of interest you may like, and I could introduce you to my friends. Have a think about it. No rush.

To: jane-hubbard@skycorres.co.uk
From: daisyduke71@gomail.com
Date: Sunday, 16th August 07:14

Dear Jane

Well, from your last email, I'm still reeling over Julian. I know he's your son, and I shouldn't talk out of turn, but he's a grown man. He should be supporting you at a time like this. He should be taking your side, the innocent side. The way Derek treated you has been terrible; does he not see that? What is it with men? They think it's okay to treat women no better than rotten fruit. Well, at least the fruit is given a squeeze now and again. He should have tripped over his lip when he left your house, it might have knocked some sense into him. To be blunt, Julian is not a child. He's a married man with a wife to tell him he's a spoilt brat and a child on the way that will eventually rival him for the title. Do not waste any more time trying to call him. Believe me, he'll soon come running back to the only parent who has time for him if he thinks he's at risk of losing her as well.

I get that it's a shock for Julian. I mean, to think that you've spent your whole life being the only child to then find out you have a little brother who recently enjoyed a jaunt to the Cayman Islands is enough to make anyone feel slightly miffed. Was he dramatic as a child? Our Cheryl could turn herself purple if we dared to walk past the Petit Filous aisle. I can still hear her screaming now when I go down there to get my Yakults. My advice is to let them all get on with it.

You have enough to get over without taking on their dramas as well.

In other news, I have a week off next week. I would have loved to have gone down South for a few days, but I promised our Cheryl I would have the kiddies while she and Kelvin decorate the kids' bedrooms. She's moving them all around. She had Sharpay and Troy in their own room and our Bruno and Beyoncé in the other. But Bruno is getting a bit old now, so they've decided to put the boys together in the back room and the girls together in the front. Cheryl and Kelvin are taking the small bedroom. The kids have so much stuff they need the bigger rooms. I've paid for new bunk beds for them and new bedding. I also said I'd get the carpets and help with the paint. Cheryl and Kelvin are buying new lampshades, nameplates for the door and a new box for all the McDonald's toys they have. Kelvin reckons they could be worth a few bob one day, but what anyone would want with a Ronald McDonald puppet glove, a pair of sunglasses with a missing lens and a Mario Kart with no wheels, I've no idea. He keeps saying someone else's junk is someone else's treasure, but I said that only applied on the *Antiques Roadshow*, not to the tat shat out by a fast-food outlet. I'm beginning to suspect Kelvin's mum and dad were also brother and sister.

Maybe I'll come down in the autumn. I still have a few days left to take before the end of the year. I could possibly combine it with a bit of Christmas shopping. I'll see how things go.

In the meantime, get yourself out. See if your mate who works on the make-up counter fancies a night out. Julie, is it? The sooner you have some good male company in your life, the sooner you'll stop worrying about the lousy male company you're currently putting up with.

Lots of love

Daisy

xxx

To: daisyduke71@gomail.com
From: jane-hubbard@skycorres.co.uk
Date: Sunday, 23rd August 15:41

Dear Daisy

I hope you enjoyed your week off. The weather wasn't great, which was a shame. I often thought about you and wondered how you would keep the little ones amused. But seeing your creative skills on the ship and what you did with that map of Buenos Aries as you sang 'Don't Cry for Me Argentina' to the family from Guildford left me with the confidence that a good time was probably had by all.

I still haven't heard from Julian. However, I have heard from Carrie, who said he went back to work on Wednesday, as his boss was getting impatient with him. It's high season for holidays, even when you are overweight. His boss said if fat people, who have more to be depressed about, can haul their arses around the Brecon Beacons, then Julian could get his arse over to Ringwood, otherwise, he would be giving him another warning. I pushed Carrie on 'another', and apparently, he already had a warning three months ago when he manhandled a man with a rucksack, as he thought was a terrorist entering the building, but it turned out it was the new rep from the insurance company who'd lost his visitor's pass.

I haven't heard from Derek either. I was going to text him, but then I realised I had nothing to say to him. I just feel the need to contact him, and I don't know why. It's a habit that I need to break. I was the same when the cleaner left. I would call her periodically just to ask her how to remove various stains from my Indian rug. I guess if he wants me, he knows where I am.

Anyway, I took your advice and called Julie, and we did indeed go for cocktails. She didn't need much persuading, so we went to the local wine bar on Friday night. To be honest, there are a few just along the high street. We'd planned to visit them all, but in the second one, Ancora, we met a couple of lovely gentlemen. They were here for a friend's wedding and had stayed for the weekend. We hadn't planned to spend the whole evening with them, but when we made some noise about moving on, they looked upset. I don't know what possessed me, but in the end, I asked them to join us in Jackson's, where we stayed for the rest of the night.

His name is Himesh. He's from London, and he's a creative designer. He's a couple of years younger than me. He's been divorced for a couple of years, has no children, owns his own house and drives a seven-series BMW. Quite a catch. Well, he took my number, and my phone has been pinging ever since. He went to the wedding yesterday and asked me to pop in, but I said no. He said the wedding party was huge and the bride and groom wouldn't mind an extra one, but I still declined. He had to return to London today but called me from the M3. We chatted for a long time. He talked of his ex-wife and how they were still on good terms. She's since married again, and he seems genuinely happy for her. I gave him the edited highlights of my life with Derek, including all the latest shenanigans. He sounded appalled, to be honest with you. At the end of the call, he asked when he could see me again, and I said we should wait and see how things go. There's no rush. I'll keep you up to date if there are any developments.

Jane

x

To: jane-hubbard@skycorres.co.uk
From: daisyduke71@gomail.com
Date: Monday, 24th August 20:54

Dear Jane

I've just sat down and thought I would pour myself a glass of Prosecco and catch up with you. I'm glad to have a bit of normality back in my life. As you know, I had the kiddies over last week. Never again. I was absolutely exhausted. I'm too old to be looking after little ones now for that length of time. The weather was terrible here, too, so I had a right time trying to keep them amused. But it was nice to see some of the old classics are still popular, like making dens and baking cakes.

Bruno wasn't much trouble. He just wanted to play on his Nintendo thing, and all our Beyoncé wanted to do was play with hair. It's a shame our Sharpay hasn't got much left since the chewing gum accident; otherwise, Beyoncé would've been amused for hours. Our Troy is a little sod, though. He upset Mrs Pemberton next door when he asked why she was wearing a coat made of cats. (She was wearing her faux fur.) He then went on to have a piss in a puddle outside Jim's house over the road. Jim dragged him back to ours, none too pleased. Our Troy said he just wanted to make the puddles yellow instead of mucky colour. The thing is, he doesn't like using the toilets in my house, as the one upstairs is a macerator and makes a shocking noise. The worst thing I did was try to explain how they work, and now he permanently walks around upstairs with his hands cupping his willy. I don't think he had a poo the whole time he was here, and when I drove him home, I swear I heard him panting on the back seat.

I wasn't happy when I got to Cheryl's. The bunk beds were only half-built. The new carpet had a tea stain on it already, which I managed to clean out, and the painted walls looked like they'd been dried with a towel. Cheryl said her and Kelvin had not been well for most of the week and had had to stay in bed. I roared at the pair of them and ended up staying there until late last night so we could get the rooms finished. Our Cheryl insisted she would finish the jobs if I took the kids back with me. But I had to remind her that I have a job and I also didn't think the neighbours could take another week of them. Kelvin said he could have a relapse any minute, and when I asked him his symptoms, he said a runny nose, sore eyes, swelling of the face and a headache. I told him that he had anything from hay fever to the bubonic plague, so the sooner we got the bunk beds up, the better. I heard him saying to our Cheryl that I was a heartless bitch.

I didn't leave until after eleven, telling them that the heartless woman had bought all of their new school uniforms, and they were in the bags, ready to be hung up. Then our Cheryl asked if I had sewn the name tags in. I told her I had, as I had managed to find time somewhere in between me being a bitch, making a Lancashire hotpot and turning Amish.

I will admit, Jane. I was seething as I drove home, and then there was no relief when I got home as the place was a tip, and there wasn't a thing to eat in the cupboards. By the time I got back, it was too late to go to the shops, and I was shattered, so I went straight to bed. I then threw another sicky with work today. I just needed a day to sort myself out. Maybe I've caught the plague from Kelvin, the cheeky bastard.

So, I spent the day getting the house straight and then had a nice bath. Dean wanted to come over, but I've barely got the energy to get my legs upstairs, never mind my leg over. He hasn't seen me for over a week, so I'm sure he would be up for a session bordering Olympic levels. He has a very high sex drive.

Talking of sex, how fit do you think Himesh is? And why are you taking things slowly? What are you waiting for? Just get out there! Whether that's with Himesh or back out with Julie to find your next prey. Ha-ha. But you have to admit, Jane, that male attention is good for the soul. I never thought I would be with another man again. Maybe I should start doing yoga like you so I can be nimble enough for the positions he throws me in.

Keep me up to date with all the details.

Lots of love

Daisy

xxx

To: daisyduke71@gomail.com
From: jane-hubbard@skycorres.co.uk
Date: Saturday, 29th August 15:41

Dear Daisy

Sorry I haven't been in touch all week. I've been busy keeping fit (since your yoga comment), getting myself waxed from the neck down (I hear that's the fashion now) and shopping for new clothes. My friend, Julie, said my wardrobe was a little on the stuffy side, and unless I was applying for a job at Number Ten, I could loosen up my style a bit. So, I went out and spent the whole day in Southampton with Julie in tow. She helped me spend over £600 and treated me to afternoon tea on the way home. Even if I don't see Himesh, I thoroughly enjoyed my day out with her.

He texted me and wants to meet next Friday, but I'm not sure. I asked him would he be driving back to London after the date, and he said no, he would be getting a hotel in the area. I'm not sure if he wanted me to ask him to stay here. Can you imagine Mrs Pemberton next door if I had a man stepping over the threshold? It's all a bit quick, don't you think? I might put him off for another week or two or until I can master the Pigeon pose in yoga.

It's a shame you didn't have such a good week with the kids. I do hope Cheryl and Kelvin realise and appreciate how much you do for them. I'm not so sure that Carrie and Julian will let me have such an active role in my new grandchild's life. I may hold off researching schools in their catchment area until such time as I ascertain how involved I am.

Does that sound selfish? I could maybe do a small spreadsheet of the top ten according to Ofsted on their facilities and feeder schools. But no more than that.

Anyway, I must dash. I have the vicar coming over to discuss Harvest Festival. I think he may want me to organise the food collection. Last year, Floella sorted it. How the poor felt about receiving a gallon of truffle oil, quinoa, umpteen packets of orzo, and a large sack of risotto rice is anyone's guess.

Speak soon.

Jane

x

To: jane-hubbard@skycorres.co.uk
From: daisyduke71@gmail.com
Date: Monday, 31st August 22:12

Dear Jane

I hope you had a nice weekend. How did it go with the vicar, and what the hell is quinoa?

Well, I've had a right week. My sister Ruth has been looking after Dad since he was diagnosed with dementia. He can look after himself most days, but when he's bad, his mind is stuck somewhere between 1981 and 1991. The doctors have said it's quite common for people to revert to a time gone by. It's just his episodes are getting more frequent and lasting longer. Ruth has always been a brilliant nurse with him, and with me working, it made sense for him to go to her. But lately, her husband Colin has said they can no longer look after him. Colin says Ruth needs to make him his priority now, seeing as his gout is playing him up more and more.

Colin's just bone idle, the truth be told, and he loses his patience with Dad over the TV. Dad was trying to find Frank Bough on *Nationwide* while Colin was watching *Tipping Point*. He said that was the last straw. So, it looks like I have no choice but to have my dad with me. I spoke to the staff in work today and said I may have to leave, but they may be able to look at me taking on more admin duties and working from home instead. Dr Halsey said they couldn't lose me after all the years of loyal service I've given them, and that they'd somehow try and cobble a role together. I must admit, I felt very guilty about all the sickies I've taken lately. They said they'd let me know this week.

If I can, I'll have Dad move in here, but if not, we may have to look at putting him in a home. Colin is determined to throw him out, and Ruth is too timid to stand up to him. I don't know where she gets all this mildness from. Dad worked for Bentley out in Crewe and was quite active with the unions. Mum was very independent and ran her own tea shop for over thirty years. I think Colin has literally bored the life out of our Ruth. But she won't be told.

So Himesh? Why are you putting him off? He only wants to take you out. You don't have to have him around the house if you don't want to, but I can't understand why. He sounds gorgeous. You've got to crack that Easter Egg at some point, and why not fill it with a bit of Eastern Promise? Just tell him to come up and get him to book the nearest Travelodge and see how you feel by the end of the night. I'm sure your mate Julie would agree with me. You have to jump on the horse at some point, and I'm fairly sure he won't give a hoot if you can do the Pigeon pose. You don't want to pull all your best moves the first time, anyway. You build up to wrapping your ankles around the back of your head for times when he takes you for dirty weekends away and a West End show. Dean didn't even know I had a bean bag until he took me to the Michelin-starred restaurant out Cheshire way.

Just call him and have a little fun.

Lots of love

Daisy

xxx

Dear Daisy

Is there a full moon? What is going on in the world? Let me tell you about the week I've just had. So, Dominic, the vicar, came over last Saturday to discuss the Harvest Festival in the church. He was very gushing about my involvement with the summer fête, which was minimal, really. All I did was sort the trestle tables in the large marquee and keep old Mr Robinson away from the gas heaters, as he has a tendency to sway due to him consuming at least half a dozen pints of scrumpy by lunchtime. He's harmless most of the time, but throw in a hay bale seating area, and you're asking for trouble.

Anyway, the vicar came over and asked whether I was interested in taking a more prominent role with this type of thing, and I said I would think about it. He then 'popped' over unannounced on Wednesday to see if I'd made up my mind. He was quite insistent on coming in even when I said I was tackling the grouting in the en suite. He then proceeded to make himself at home, making tea and opening a packet of garibaldis I was saving for when Carrie and Julian came over.

While dunking his biscuit, he started asking me about Derek and how painful everything must have been for me. When I revealed the length and depth of Derek's deception, he took my hand and said there was obviously a plan for me, and God would show me what this plan was, but he, the vicar, knew it would be a better life for me. I said I hoped a tiler was part of God's plan as the grouting was defeating me, and I suspected new tiles might be better. He left after that, and I thought no more of it, except for when I went shopping in Waitrose to replace the garibaldis. And I forgot to ask him about me considering Buddhism and shaving my head.

He came over again today, looking very different. He looked quite casual, even wearing a training shoe, I noted. He came in again, and when I rushed to place myself in between him and the biscuit cupboard, he took it as a pass at him, and he made a lunge to kiss me! I pushed him away, and he looked very embarrassed and said he thought that was what I wanted! Whatever gave him that impression is beyond me. Surely, opening the front door in your Cath Kidston apron should be interpreted as a clear sign of sex non grata. Who knew a rosebud-covered pinny could induce such sexual tension, especially from a vicar?!

I told him to leave immediately, but then he started saying how much he admired me and how he had always had feelings for me. Apparently, he's felt like this since I dressed up as Carmen Miranda promoting 'Eat your Five a Day' on a stall at the Easter Fair. I told Julie the coconuts were a step too far for Lymington, especially in April, but she said no one would come to the stall anyway, seeing as Bertie had his bonbon stall by the bouncy castle. Anyway, Dominic said every time he sees me, he keeps seeing me as a sexy fruit basket. I eventually got him out of the house, but the whole time he was saying he wouldn't give up and he would be back soon!

You'd think all of that praying and being on your knees for most of the day would dampen any sexual desire. Since I ejected him from the house, I've had a bottle of Prosecco, a large Pernod, and nothing to eat, so forgive me if nothing is making sense. I've also binned my apron in case it heightens his sexual desire.

With regard to Himesh, I have accepted a dinner invitation for next Friday. Do you think I should tell him about Dominic? He's only just getting his head around Derek. Sorry for burdening you with all of this with all that you have on your plate. Your dad does sound like a handful. Are you sure you would be able to look after him and work as well? That seems an awful lot to take on. Will Cheryl be able to help you? It's a shame the grandkids aren't a little older, as they could also pitch in. Will his dementia deteriorate more? In the sense that his periods will be longer, not that he reverts to other decades. Would your mind being stuck in the seventies be deemed a sign of deterioration?

I'm not medically minded and remember very little of the seventies, so I can offer no opinion on the matter. I'm sure you're well informed, especially with your role in the doctor's surgery. I would love to say I could help, but my only nursing of a mental health issue was when Julian thought he had PTSD after witnessing an unfortunate accident with a supermarket employee and a rogue chain of thirty trolleys. He would only shop in the Metro store after that, saying he was unlikely to see anyone with a trolley in a local convenience store. Carrie eventually gave him therapy by pointing out that he was spending a least twelve per cent more on his shop by going there instead of the large supermarket, and anyone pushing more than thirty trolleys would have been asking for trouble. After calling the store, at my suggestion, about their H & S policy and being pacified with their trolley practices, he now will patronise the local Asda.

Anyway, I'll sign off now. I either need another glass of fizz or I need to go to bed as I'm starting to sober up.

Jane

x

P.S. Quinoa is a grain.

To: jane-hubbard@skycorres.co.uk
From: daisyduke71@gomail.com
Date: Tuesday, 8th September 18:46

Dear Jane

Well, I felt quite breathless reading your last email. Get you spreading your allure all over Hampshire. You shouldn't underestimate the power of an apron. Why do you think all of those French maids get chased all over the place? Take that apron away, and she looks like she could be in mourning. The apron is what makes it so appealing. So, I suggest, in future, answer the door in anything with an elasticated waistband. Nothing makes you sexy if it has an expandable middle, believe me.

Lunging and lusting aside, is Dominic a contender? You know what men are like. Once they get all that pent-up sexual frustration out of the way, you tend to find a very different man emerges. My James came out of the other side finding contentment in *Match of the Day*, the odd Jack Daniel's and a decent carbonara. By the time he reached his forties, he was very chilled, and the only time I saw him get frustrated was when he was challenged with a stubborn lid on a jar of piccalilli. The sex was still very satisfying but a little predictable, but that's life with the same partner of thirty-odd years, I suppose. But another way of looking at it is all that flirting could be an aperitif to a sexually adventurous man, and let's face it, you could do with a flurry of ferment. And there was me thinking all vicars were full of prayer and Ovaltine. How wrong I was.

Well, news about Dad, he had a lucid moment yesterday and told Ruth that he didn't want to be a burden and would go in a home. She then said to him that he could move in with me and that I wanted to look after him. She said he seemed pleased with that before he got distracted by Colin eating grapes. Dad began shouting that they had better not come from Argentina after what they did to *HMS Sheffield*. Colin pacified him, saying they were French grapes, to which Dad said that was okay as he didn't mind François Mitterrand and thought he was a decent bloke, even for a Frog. So it looks like he'll be moving in with me sooner rather than later, as Colin has already started boxing up his belongings. When I said maybe the idea should settle with Dad first, he said surely Dad would have to remember in the first place for anything to settle. I suppose he does have a point.

Our Cheryl isn't happy about the idea. She said she wasn't sure if she could trust Dad around the kids. I said as long as they don't go around the house saying they love Thatcher, Culture Club or Prince Edward (he doesn't mind the other Royals), then all would be fine. She then asked where the kids were supposed to sleep if he was taking the second bedroom. I told her we could still get the bunk beds in the box room and buy a camp bed for the other two. She didn't like that idea, so I told her straight that the kids have a camp bed or no bed. I also told her that the kids wouldn't be able to sleep over as often as they have been, as I would have enough on my plate.

She went on saying her Aunt Ruth was selfish and wrecking her life, as she wouldn't be able to go out when she wanted. I told her she might want to take that up with her

Uncle Colin. She declined this suggestion, of course, as she knew her Uncle Colin would bounce her out of the house. Colin and Cheryl have never seen eye to eye. He says I've spoilt her and indulged her all her life. He may be right; I do struggle to say no to her sometimes, but she was my only child and sometimes my only company when her dad was too tired to do stuff. But she isn't a child anymore. She's a mum and needs to sort out her life and priorities.

Other news is I think I might be going off Dean. I may be being a little fussy, but I'm starting to notice things about him that irritate me a bit. For instance, he is a very noisy eater. We went to a restaurant the other day, and he had corn on the cob. It was like watching a beaver chewing on a log. That, with the dripping butter, made for a very noisy spectacle, I can tell you. The other thing is his toilet habits. He never shuts the door! I don't want to see him mid-stream while he scratches his arse, and I certainly don't want to watch him seated while I try and sort out the airing cupboard. James and I were not shy with our toilet habits, but it took a few years and a baby to be 'optional' with the lock on the door. This guy's only known me for five minutes, and I know he's a folder, not a scruncher, with the toilet paper, and he doesn't know what the brush is for at the side. Some of the devastation I've had to deal with has made me miss a few dates. No one wants to go to the local tandoori house when you've just been tackling the Armitage Shanks, even if you are armed with Domestos. The other thing that annoys me is his incessant talk of plants, soil, and growing aids. I know he has a garden centre and it's a big part of his life, but I really don't need to know the different grades of manure while I'm trying to watch *The One Show* over a bowl of chilli con carne.

I think I'll just see. Maybe see him less and less, and then eventually, he'll realise that I'm trying to keep him at arm's length. Or do you think I should just rip that Band-Aid off and be done with it? I haven't finished with a man for decades. Is there a right way to do it these days? Things change so much with each generation, and I'm not sure I'm keeping up. Our Cheryl said men these days are clued up about Slimming World, stain removal and the love life of Fern Britton. Though, why a man would be interested in the last point is beyond me. I've always found Holly Willoughby far more entertaining.

Now back to your love life. I suggest you keep your mouth shut about Dominic and Himesh to either of them. You're only going out on dates, and to be brutally honest, it could all fizzle out after a couple of them. I would also be careful about how much you talk about Derek. No date wants to hear all about the ex, whether negative or positive. My husband is dead, and even Dean curled his lip when I mentioned that James had a slight addiction to Monster Munch. No, keep them all in their own little toy boxes, and then you can just play with them when you want.

Let me know how the date goes on Friday. I'm all about the detail, so don't be hanging back on me.

Lots of love

Daisy

xxx

To: daisyduke71@gomail.com
From: jane-hubbard@skycorres.co.uk
Date: Saturday, 12th September 18:14

Dear Daisy

Well, I couldn't wait to tell you about my date with Himesh last night. I would have emailed you when I came home, but by the time I took off my Spanx and realised I'd lost two nails in the process, I was too exhausted to fire up the Mac. So, he took me to a beautiful Indian restaurant called The Corridor and introduced me to some wonderful dishes, including black cod that had been cooked in a banana leaf. He was so knowledgeable about the menu, which impressed me. I was quite taken aback when he asked was the lamb from Wales, and when they said it was from Scotland, he looked disappointed and opted for the guinea fowl instead. Is there a difference? Apparently so, according to Himesh, and he laughed at the question but didn't answer it. Would you know the difference?

I took your advice and didn't mention Derek or Dominic at all. I then realised that I have very little going on in my life and struggled to talk to him. Once I'd told him about the grandchild on the way and my failure with my bonsai tree, I didn't know what else to talk about. Am I really that boring? Is that why Derek left me for someone more vibrant? I bet Olivia has lots of friends, hobbies, and past lovers. I'm not sure I'll go out with him again unless I find time to find more friends or learn a new hobby. I always wanted to learn how to make candles, but Derek told me that it was unlikely we would experience the blackouts of the seventies, so what was the point? When I said that they could be used to diffuse a room, he asked why did the angels invent windows then?

Even with a creative lie, I'm sure that if Himesh ever took me to bed, he would know that any past audience of me taking my bra off was very limited.

So, there you have it. No gory details because I now realise I am very dull. Maybe I should encourage the vicar. What do you think? I just feel Himesh might be too full of life for me.

Jane

x

To: jane-hubbard@skycorres.co.uk
From: daisyduke71@gomail.com
Date: Saturday, 19th September 22:11

Dear Jane

Sorry for the late reply. I've had a busy week. The new carpet was laid this week by a couple of men who were either colour-blind, stupid or taking the piss. I'd picked a nice shade of brown, a bit like Blake Carrington's face from *Dynasty*. Anyway, I went upstairs and left them to it. When they called me down to check the job, the carpet was bottle green! I told the men that I'd picked a shade similar to Blake's face, and one of them said that this colour was a day when he was jealous. When I argued, they said it was the nearest shade they had to what I picked.

After a few choice words and an unopened purse, they had it back up, and the right one was laid the following day. Mrs Pemberton said that the firm was notorious for trying to lay their offcuts, and in her friend's house, they once laid a carpet that had been used in the local casino. She said every time her husband sat to eat at the dinner table, he would ask for his dinner to be put on black.

Anyway, I've re-read your last email and must admit you sound boring as hell. But I've met you and know that you're not. Let me start by saying that Derek did not leave you because he thought you were boring. He left you because he's an arsehole. As with most men, they think the grass is greener on the other side, but they fail to realise that new grass needs a lot more attention than a well-established and more mature lawn shall we say. Now regarding Himesh, if he's asked you on a second date, then I'm sure he found you interesting enough. There's been more to your life than the last month or two. Maybe I was wrong in saying you shouldn't mention Derek. He was a big part of your life, and glossing over it all might look like you're hiding something.

The vicar, to be honest, sounds a hoot. Randy, yes, but still a hoot. He might be worth keeping on the back burner if only to give you something to talk about and keep the garibaldi biscuit factory in business. Sometimes I think you'd make a good vicar's wife. You're aware of the community calendar, drive a Mercedes and probably know who the patron saint of handbags is. Then I think maybe not, as the altar wine would take a hammering. (Remember the day we disembarked at Key West and nearly missed going to Cuba? All because of the wine that tasted like Ribena Tooth Kind.) Also, you're not particularly good with anything botanical, and a vicar's wife needs to be an artist when it comes to flower arranging. Let's see how that naturally pans out, eh?

My news is I have been avoiding Dean for a few days. I was hoping he would get the hint and maybe finish with me, but Jade, Cheryl's mate from the garden centre, said he talks about me all the time and was heard saying he wished he'd met me years ago. I'm not sure he would have gotten as far with me back then as he has now. When I was younger, I was more attracted to the bad boy. I once had a whirlwind romance with a young man who drove an XR3i, wore an earring and never paid a penny Poll Tax. Someone with ambitions of opening a garden centre would not have made it far with me. Those men likely grew up thinking Wall's Vienetta was sophisticated and had a lot of 'alone' time with a picture of Princess Michael of Kent. I may have to take the bull by the horns on that one. Seems a bit cruel to prolong the agony.

Daddy is moving in next week. He is practically packed, courtesy of Colin, of course. I'd take him sooner, but my hours are not being cut until then. I was talking to Mrs Pemberton from next door, and she kindly offered to give me a hand with him with things like watching him while I run to the supermarket. Cheryl said she would help, but I'm not sure I can rely on her. Shame I have more faith in the old biddy next door than my own daughter. I don't know much about Mrs Pemberton except she does all her washing on a Saturday and cooks everything in a pressure cooker. Having her on hand will help enormously, if only how to show me how to cook a ham in twenty minutes. Dad loves ham.

I know this Christmas is going to be a challenge with him and our Cheryl with the kids. I hope they all get on and Cheryl doesn't get too frustrated when he insists on listening to the King's speech. I might have to do a trick that Colin does. Last year, Dad had polished off half a bottle of advocaat by one o'clock, so when he settled for a little nap, Colin changed all the clocks. By the time he woke up, he thought he'd missed it. They even had him in bed by nine (Dad thought it was half ten). I'm not sure if I'll be able to get away with it with the kids in the house. I don't mind the King, to be honest. For all his money, I wouldn't want his life. I'm stressing already about the neighbour helping out. Imagine having a legion of servants to look after.

Well, I must go now. Keep me updated about all your man troubles, you lucky thing.

Love Daisy

xxx

To: daisyduke71@gomail.com
From: jane-hubbard@skycorres.co.uk
Date: Friday, 2nd October 19:10

Dear Daisy

Sorry, it's been a while since I've been in touch. No doubt you've been busy moving your dad in the last week. I've been busy too. First, Carrie asked me to be her birth partner, which I'm thrilled about. She said Julian had declined the offer after hearing a colleague go into great detail about his daughter's birth and how it had scarred him for life. He and the mother divorced a year after the child was born, citing 'post-traumatic stress which was enhanced by a shaven undercarriage and an unsympathetic ear'. Julian, being very thoughtful, said he didn't want them to go through a similar experience so thought it best she ask one of the grandmothers-in-waiting for support. Carrie's mother discovered veganism when Carrie was fifteen and went to live in a commune in the South of France. Carrie is still heartbroken at the abandonment, and when I said she should reach out and tell her mother that Waitrose does a fine selection of plant-based products, she politely refused. So by the process of elimination, I'm next in line. I don't mind being third.

Being her birth partner means I have to attend her birth classes. We go once a week to the hospital where she is giving birth. The class is run by a lady called Esther, who has had three children herself, so in my opinion, she is more than qualified to give advice. We've only been to one class so far, and that was just a tour of the labour ward, which I was highly impressed with. Things have come a long way since I gave birth to Julian on a plastic mattress and with nothing to take the pain away except a tank of gas and air and an old copy of *Woman's Own*.

Carrie has decided to have a water birth. It seems this is acceptable even if you haven't got any swimming badges, as you give birth in a small pool which you can sit in. It's not a requirement that the baby can swim either, which is a relief. Esther said we would look at alternative births later in the course. Julian said he's glad I'm going with Carrie, so it seems we've made up now. He said it's about support, but he also said he would be grateful if I could encourage her to leave things as nature intended. Why he can't tell his wife to stop shaving her bikini line is beyond me. Is this the only reason he's started talking to me again?

My other news is Himesh has asked me out on a date for tomorrow night. I have accepted, as I think he may find the whole progression of birth choices fascinating, and I also have a lovely new Hobbs dress that I wouldn't mind taking for a spin. We're going for another meal, but he said I could pick this time. So I've booked a table at a restaurant halfway between my house and the hotel where he's staying. He's in the Castle Keep this time. He said staying in the Travelodge was an experience he would not like to repeat, and any hotel that bolts the shampoo to the wall suggests a clientele he wouldn't want to mingle with. He did, however, praise their breakfast and gave a fair review on TripAdvisor highlighting their hash browns. I'll let you know if the second date was a success.

I've not heard from Derek for a while and have not asked Julian how things are with him either. Whenever I think of him, I feel so betrayed and foolish. I don't feel comfortable with either of these emotions, so I don't wallow too much. When I do think of him, I think of Olivia more and what she sees in him. He's so much older than her. Maybe she's just after his money.

Well, I'm off now. Have a good weekend and let me know how things are going with your father.

Jane

x

To: jane-hubbard@skycorres.co.uk
From: daisyduke71@gomail.com
Date: Monday, 5th October 20:08

Dear Jane

Don't apologise for not replying sooner. To be honest with you, I've hardly had a chance to look at my emails since Dad moved in. Oh, Jane, I'm not so sure I am going to be able to cope with him. Trying to convince him that some things aren't available anymore is a nightmare. On Sunday, he asked me to get him a copy of the *News of The World*, which I had to tell him they didn't print anymore because of a phone-tapping scandal. He blamed Thatcher, saying it was her fault because she privatised BT, and that's why he couldn't get his paper. He still has some lucid moments every now and again, but they're getting shorter and shorter. I think he was a bit frightened when he realised he'd moved in with me, but I managed to tell him we were getting on fine before he went to the kitchen looking for Mum.

Cheryl came around wanting me to babysit the first night he was there. I know it sounds wicked to say, but I'm sure she only brought them that night to show him that her kids come first. I had to tell her plain that Dad was my priority, and I would look after the kids anytime she was stuck, not bored! I offered to take them to the zoo for a few hours. That way, Dad could come too. But she said she didn't want the kids coming home smelling like elephant shit. It's got nothing to do with the animals at all. It's the fact that I said I would take them during the day and not the night when her and Kelvin can get smashed on cheap lager and wine.

I was so annoyed when she left. Not once did she ask me how I was getting on, managing to work from home and look after her grandad. It would have been nice to tell her that he had asked about her the day before while he was watching *Little Britain*. Most of the time, he doesn't know who she is, never mind the little ones. When they all piled in, he locked himself in the bathroom and said he wouldn't come out until my friend was gone with her rug rats. It's a good job Cheryl didn't hear that.

I've been keeping Dean at arm's length as well. I keep telling him that I'm busy, but you know as well as I do that his number is up. It was very nice while it lasted, but it didn't last long, a bit like your garibaldi supply. I will need to have a chat with him soon and let him down gently. I don't even know how to end it in this day and age. The last person I split up with was a young lad from Eccleston. I met him in the street on the way to the chippy, and when he asked if he could come with me, I told him no and that I would be buying a fishcake for one, now and for the foreseeable. He took the hint and jumped the bus back home. I met James the following week at a local club, and the rest, as they say, is history.

How are things with Dominic? Isn't it Harvest Festival around now? Is he keeping you on your toes? And Himesh? Your allure must be at an all-time high and all wrapped up in a Hobbs dress. Get you! My new hours are going well, and working from home has its pros and cons. The pros are I can get an extra half hour in bed, and as long as I keep UK Gold so he can watch a bit of *Juliet Bravo*, then Dad's happy. The cons are I'm too near the fridge, I miss working with people, and there's only so much of the *Juliet Bravo* theme tune I can take. I'm sure I'll get used to the new routine, though. Dr Bridges, head of the practice, pops in now and again to make sure I'm okay. He doesn't need to, as Paula, the office manager, checks in a lot and gives me my work. It's all admin now. I do a few calls, but not many, which is a shame, as some older patients don't like talking to the younger staff. I don't think they feel they get any sympathy talking about a prolapsed womb with a girl who still wears a thong.

It's great news about you being Carrie's birth partner. I saw Cheryl give birth to our Bruno and Beyoncé. By the time she had the twins, I had kind of gotten over it. She had a caesarean in the end.

Well, I must go. Dad's shouting for me to make him some supper. Let me know about your date with Himesh.

Lots of love

Daisy

xx

To: daisyduke71@gomail.com
From: jane-hubbard@skycorres.co.uk
Date: Sunday, 11th October 15:42

Dear Daisy

Thanks for your encouraging words about my allure. My date with Himesh was a success, and we shared a deeply passionate kiss. He insisted he walked me home and didn't make any move to come in. To be honest, if he had tried, I think I would have let him. It's only the second date, but I feel I know so much about him because we talk all the time on the phone. The meal was nice. I was a bit nervous about booking the restaurant, as he seems to know his food, and his knowledge of wine is breathtaking. The only thing was he didn't finish his dessert. I continued to tell him about the water birth plan while I finished off his lemon posset.

He called this morning before he headed back to London. I cooked him Eggs Florentine, but instead of spinach, I used iceberg lettuce, as it was all I had. I'm not sure it worked. He didn't eat much of it because he'd already had breakfast back at the hotel. (He'd forgotten I said I would cook, apparently.) Before he left, he invited me to London next weekend. He said his apartment was big enough, and I could stay in his spare room.

Do you think it's a ploy, though? What if I get there, he locks me up, and I become his sex slave? I don't think all of that pushing and shoving will do my bones any good. The doctor says I have early signs of osteoporosis. He could literally reduce me to talc while he has his wicked way. What do you think? Should I go?

Jane

x

To: jane-hubbard@skycorres.co.uk
From: daisyduke71@gomail.com
Date: Monday, 12th October 19:45

Dear Jane

Where do you get these ideas from? A sex slave? You should be so lucky! If you don't want to go, then I will. He's got money, is gorgeous, and knows what Eggs Florentine is. Oh, just let him have his way with you and stop overthinking it. Have a yoghurt beforehand if you're worried about your bones.

Love Daisy

xxx

To: daisyduke71@gomail.com
From: jane-hubbard@skycorres.co.uk
Date: Sunday, 18th October 18:02

Dear Daisy

Well, I took your advice and went to London. I drove the Mercedes in case I needed to make a quick getaway, which thankfully was not necessary. I arrived on Saturday around lunchtime. His apartment is beautiful and overlooks the Thames. A little on the snug side, but I guess it's fine for one person. I was shown his spare bedroom, which was beautifully decorated. So lovely, in fact, I suspect a lady may have been involved in some of the design decisions. But let's not dwell on that.

Saturday day, we did a little shopping and had a spot of lunch in The Shard. I've always wanted to go there. I asked Derek to take me for my fiftieth birthday. It was then I discovered his fear of heights. He said if the angels wanted us to be that high, then why on earth did they invent bungalows? I'm starting to realise that Derek said some stupid things. Everyone knows it was probably Barrett.

After a whirl on the London Eye and some sightseeing, we went back to his and changed for the evening. I wore a very daring red dress from Reiss and shaved my legs. I know you may laugh at that, but me shaving my legs means I'm mentally throwing myself at him. We then went for a lighter bite before we headed to the theatre to watch *Mamma Mia*. The show was incredible, even though I was sat by a man who tucked into a Tupperware bowl of what looked and smelled like leftover chicken chow mein. Why on earth would anyone bring such a fiddly dish to eat to the theatre? Surely a low-odour sandwich would have been a better choice and a far quieter eating option while they sang 'I Have a Dream'.

After the theatre, we headed back to his place and had a little nightcap, and then I went to bed. Well, I say bed. I made it as far as my bedroom door, where he asked if he could tuck me in. I said yes, but as you can guess, there was no tucking in. All I will say is that it was one of the best nights of my life, he's a very generous lover, and I'm glad I continued with the yoga. When I woke up this morning, he was already up and had gone to the gym. I told him I wanted to leave by midday, so by the time I'd showered, made the bed, had three cups of coffee, tidied the lounge, deadheaded some of his plants and made myself some breakfast while waiting for him, we didn't have long left. He'd been caught at the gym by a client, and the time just ran away. So we had a quick chat while he put my bag in the car, and I was soon on the road. I think he may have had an appointment to attend, as I got the impression he needed me gone, which is fine.

I must admit by the time I got home, I was exhausted, so I had a little nap. Since I woke up, I cannot stop thinking about him. He is so very different to Derek. The way he moves, the way he talks, even the way he smells, which is divine, by the way. I do wonder what he sees in me. Anyway, since returning home, I've made some decisions. The first is to change my bedding. Himesh's bedding was the best

Egyptian cotton. I have a lovely set from Debenhams, but it may be a little dated now. Also on the list is to up my yoga sessions for obvious reasons, and finally, I'm going to wait for him to call or text me first. I tend to find that I'm the first to initiate any conversation, but after giving him what can most certainly be described as a very satisfying night, he can come begging me if he wants more.

I'm very tempted to tell Julian, who may pass the information on to his father. I would love Derek to find out he was mediocre in bed, but I'm not sure how Julian will react, knowing his father's past performance or the fact that his mother has taken on another lover. I may ask Carrie about it when we go to the next birthing class. Next week is about massaging your perineum, which could prove to be a handy segue.

In response to your email, the Harvest Festival is next week. I conceded the collection of food back to Floella. Apparently, according to her, she already has some food collected and stored in appropriate facilities, including alkalised water, sprouted millet, activated almonds, emu meatballs and enough liquorice root tea to eradicate any symptoms of foot and mouth disease in the next two counties. I was shouted down by her and her sycophantic group when I said we should look at more basic food items. She responded that if the needy need anything else, they only have to go online and order Ocado delivery.

I do hope you're coping okay with your father. I do admire your multitasking abilities and the fact you're still working while he's under your feet. I only wish I had your tenacity and resilience. I wasn't too fond of *Juliet Bravo* the first time around, never mind now on repeat.

I'll email you as soon as I've heard from Himesh and update you on my new bedding venture.

Jane

x

To: jane-hubbard@skycorres.co.uk

From: daisyduke71@gomail.com

Date: **Friday, 23rd October 23:33**

Dear Jane

Sorry for emailing so late. I did try to call you, but your phone went straight to answer machine. I've just finished with Dean after a huge row and wanted someone to talk to. He came around to the house earlier this evening completely unannounced after me telling him that I couldn't see him tonight. Apparently, he'd been talking to Jade, our Cheryl's best mate, in the garden centre, and she told him I was clearly avoiding him. She'd worked him up into such a state he pulled up his Transit van on my drive like he was about to do a drugs raid, then started banging on the door, shouting my name. Then Dad started shouting that the rent man was at the door and to tell him to come back next week and he'd give him double.

As soon as I opened the door, Dean barged his way in, looking for my 'other man'. He'd completely forgotten that I mentioned to him about Dad moving in. So when he found him in the armchair, he looked at me with revulsion, saying he was disgusted, and it was no wonder I'd stopped seeing him if that's what turned me on. In front of Dad!! I told him that the only person who was disgusting was him if he thinks it's acceptable to come into a bathroom while someone is showering, take a shit and want to discuss why you don't see faggots on a menu anymore.

I told him it was equally disgusting that he picked his toenails while I made breakfast, and he's put me off hash browns for the rest of my life. I then grabbed him by the shirt and threw him out telling him to find a proper car, a pair of toenail clippers and a woman with a stronger stomach than Elvis Presley. When I walked back in, all of his shirt buttons were scattered on the floor. So he's on the M60 somewhere with his shirt flapping in the wind. Dad watched him pull away from the lounge window, asking how much rent he is collecting to need a van that size.

I tried to call our Cheryl, but she was out with her mates, and I couldn't hear her, and she couldn't hear me. So then I tried to call you. You're probably in bed with Himesh and getting thrown around your bedroom by your knicker elastic. I hope so. One of us should be having fun.

I'll leave you to it. Write back when you can.

Lots of love

Daisy

xxx

To: daisyduke71@gomail.com
From: jane-hubbard@skycorres.co.uk
Date: Sunday, 25th October 20:44

Dear Daisy

I hope this email finds you in a calmer state than the one I received over the weekend—you poor thing. I'm so sorry that I didn't take your call. My phone had run out of battery, and I hadn't noticed. So have you heard from Dean since you threw him out? Did your neighbours hear anything? Will you still use his garden centre? Do you regret saying some of the things you said?

Jane

x

To: jane-hubbard@skycorres.co.uk
From: daisyduke71@gomail.com
Date: Sunday, 25th October 21:34

Dear Jane

I've not seen him or heard from him, thank God. I think if I ever see him again, I'll swing for him. Suggesting that Dad was my new man. I mean, Dad's not exactly ugly, but he was never a modern man. He looks older than his age, but that could be the dementia or because he's still styling himself on Dennis Waterman. It's a shame it turned out the way it did. I'm not sure I will ever have another relationship. Maybe James was the only one for me.

And the only thing I regret is not putting a lock on that bathroom door.

Lots of love

Daisy

xxx

To: daisyduke71@gomail.com
From: jane-hubbard@skycorres.co.uk
Date: Sunday, 25th October 22:01

Dear Daisy

You are so resilient. I think you're marvellous. I would be so scared in case the neighbours heard. You must live in a far more tolerant area. Maybe that's because you're northern. My neighbours would either have called the police due to a 'disturbance of *Countryfile*' or worse, upset the secret assassins. They turn up at your door, wearing a floral kimono, but instead of squinting through the scope of a gun, they hide behind a bowl of roasted vegetable couscous, looking for intel.

Don't be saying things about not getting another man. You're still young. You're not even sixty yet. You still have enough years to get married and settle into mediocre sex. Talking of sex, I've not heard from Himesh. I tried waiting for him to text and heard nothing. I then decided to text him on Friday and heard nothing back. So I called him Saturday and left a message. Then I thought he might be in trouble, so I called a few times and still nothing. Then I called Julie to see what she thought. She told me to call him again but withhold my number. So I called last night, and he answered the phone. As soon as I said hello, he hung up. I'm not sure what I should do now. Do you think he recognised my voice and hung up or hung up because he didn't know it was me as I had withheld my number? I could do with some proper advice, as Julie is not very forthcoming at the moment.

But that could be because she's started Weight Watchers and is distracted with her Apple watch.

In other news, the Harvest Festival was a semi-success. I eventually ended up leading the children's activities in the church hall. Most of the children were well-behaved, but the Chisholm family almost ruined it. I was in charge of judging the scarecrow puppet competition. Most of the entrants were of typical scarecrow standard. However, the Chisholm children thought it would be funny to dress their scarecrows as Ant and Dec, who performed unspeakable acts on two of the Kardashians. I managed to avoid Dominic through most of it, but he did run after me in the car park when I was heading home. He said he could see I was in a rush and would pop in when I had more time. I think it was just an excuse so he had another reason to come over. I hope it's not any time soon. I don't think I could cope with him while I'm trying to figure out what's happening with Himesh.

Please let me know what you think of it all and what your advice would be.

Jane

x

To: jane-hubbard@skycorres.co.uk
From: daisyduke71@gomail.com
Date: Tuesday, 27th October 11:58

Dear Jane

Sorry I didn't come back yesterday. Dad was having a particularly bad day. He's doing better today. We went for a walk, and I took him to Mum's grave to see if it jogged his memory at all. He was quite chatty all the way there but went noticeably quiet when we got to her headstone. I said nothing and just cleared the grass up a bit. He was quiet most of the way home until he said, "*She's not in pain anymore, is she?*" When I said no, he smiled, and that was it. I had Dad for a moment. By the time we got home and I took his coat off, he asked if Mum had enough money for the bus to get home from the bingo. He was gone. If he stayed in the past, I could cope, but when I get him for a moment, it kills me. How bad is that? Wishing my proper dad would stay buried in his condition just to make it easier for me. Please don't judge me. I do love him dearly.

I hardly see our Cheryl and the kids. She said she's scared of Dad going loopy in front of them, and he scares the kids. I told her that her grandad's dementia is a fact of life, a fact of our family, and hiding him away was not an option. I've not heard from her since I said that, but I did see Jade in the Co-Op and she said that our Beyoncé was at hers the other day and was saying she misses me. I'll give it a couple of days and maybe pop around.

Now Himesh. I'll tell you straight; I think he's giving you the runaround. He sounds like someone who likes the chase before more than the basking afterwards. There's a reason he's on his own, and you may have just discovered it. He's a prize guy shit. There was me thinking he was going to be the modern-day Omar Shariff with his penchant for eggs and lettuce. And what's wrong with Scottish lamb? He sounds like a snob to me, and anyone who can eat guinea fowl is a step away from cannibalism. The twins had one in a hutch in the garden and played with it every day until it disappeared. Kelvin said the foxes must have had it, but it was probably stolen and sold to some pretentious restaurant for the Himeshes of the world. Don't try and phone him again. Just get back in the saddle and look for someone else. Look for someone who wants what you want. Chalk this up as experience and be glad you had it with someone who knew how to shut a bathroom door and didn't permanently smell of Baby Bio.

Lots of love

Daisy

xxx

To: daisyduke71@gomail.com
From: jane-hubbard@skycorres.co.uk
Date: Thursday, 29th October 22:01

Dear Daisy

Thanks for your advice. As much as it hurts me, I think you're right. Thank God I didn't say anything to Julian. I did speak to Carrie about him, though, so maybe he knows. Well, if he does, he can't say that I was rubbing his nose in it. I'm not sure if she was listening to me when I told her about some of his moves in bed. She seemed distracted by the midwife pushing a Tiny Tears doll through a cloth vagina. She was noticeably quiet on the way home as well. I'm sure if she'd heard me, she would have commented. The only thing she did say was she might have to revise her birth plan. I have no idea what she meant by that. I hope she isn't thinking of changing her mind and having Julian in the room with us. He's too sensitive to watch the intensity of childbirth. He had nightmares for a fortnight after watching Lady Sybil die giving birth in *Downtown Abbey*.

Have you seen Cheryl yet? You must be missing the grandkids so much. My grandchild is not born yet and even I feel a constant pull and ache to be near Carrie. I have started buying a few items and have put them in the Zen room, which I've decided will become the nursery over the next few weeks. I don't need a whole room to cross my legs or to house a bonsai tree. Do you have any suggestions on how to decorate? What are children into these days? I have no idea. Would Cheryl not let you have the older ones who understand their grandfather's condition more? Maybe they could help. They might be able to play with your dad and get him away from *Juliet Bravo*. There's a blessing right there.

Anyway, I must go. The phone keeps ringing. It will no doubt be Julian in a tizz over something. Maybe he's found out his half-brother has a more extensive puppet collection than he ever had.

Jane

x

To: jane-hubbard@skycorres.co.uk
From: daisyduke71@gomail.com
Date: Sunday, 1st November 10:27

Dear Jane

Can you believe the door is still going with trick-or-treaters? They should have been here last night, but one group turned up saying it was too cold to go out last night and the next lot said they couldn't come as they had to go to their dad's this weekend and he didn't want them wandering around the halfway house he's in at the moment. When I said I had no sweets, they said they would accept money! When I told them I had no cash on me, they said they would take PayPal! I just shut the door in their face. They'll be back tomorrow collecting a 'penny for the Guy'. Not that they have a stuffed Guy for the bonfire. Last year, a kid climbed into a trolley, and they pushed him around telling him to keep still when they could see someone coming to the door. I gave them a few coppers, and when I asked how much they had raised for fireworks, they said just over a pound and that had to be used to get the trolley as their 'Guy' was tired from walking through the estate.

I went over to our Cheryl's last night. She was getting ready to go to a Halloween party. It was fancy dress but not one where you had to go as something Halloweeny. Cheryl said that's old hat and now people tend to do it like the Americans. Her and Jade have been hammering the sunbeds for a more authentic look, shall we say. So our Cheryl went as Tina Turner. She looked good in her gold tassel dress. I offered to take her, and we picked Jade up on the way.

I didn't like to ask her who she was when she got in the car. She wore a white dress that skimmed all the wrong places and a large flower behind her ear. When they got out of the car, I asked Cheryl who she was, and she said Billie Holiday. I told Cheryl Jade's top lip was too hairy for Billie Holliday and she looked more like Billy Ocean. I hope she didn't tell her.

So, I went all that way and only managed to see the kids for half an hour. I could have gone back, I suppose, but I didn't want to sit with Kelvin while he picked his feet and talked about serial killers. The worst thing our Cheryl did was get Netflix. She said it was for the kids, but every time I go around there, someone is on the screen talking about Ted Bundy. Our Troy asked the other day if he ate a lime would it dissolve his body? Kelvin told him that limes were okay and it was lye he should steer clear of. So, as I said, I went home only to find Dad trying to fry eggs still in their shells. He'd managed to butter the bread and find a plate, at least. He was quiet today, so I caught up on a bit of work and FaceTimed the kids around three. Cheryl was still in bed. She must have had a good night. Beyoncé was trying to feed Sharpay some Rice Pops, so I presume Kelvin was with her.

I've not heard from Dean, so he's definitely taken the hint. Our Cheryl said I need to get back out there, but it's a bit hard now I've got Dad. Can't exactly hook up my sex swing in case Dad comes in wanting to know what side *Bergerac* is on. Not that I have a sex swing, but you see my point. Mind you, if they are all like Dean, I would rather be on my own. It took me years to turn James into someone who wasn't hard work. I don't know if I have the energy to do all that again. You, on the other hand, are a different story. You have so much free time you could fill it with sex swings and love chairs, and you won't have your porn drowned out by someone incessantly whistling the theme tune to *Grandstand*.

We must have a chat soon about meeting up again. We did say before Christmas. I'm sure I can get my sister to mind Dad for a night or two if I give her enough notice. I can come to you this time, or we can meet halfway. Let me know.

Lots of love

Daisy

xxx

To: daisyduke71@gomail.com
From: jane-hubbard@skycorres.co.uk
Date: Thursday, 5th November 20:10

Dear Daisy

Please forgive me in advance if any parts of this email do not make sense. I took an unexpected call tonight from Derek, and my nerves were in such a state I had to open a bottle of Chenin Blanc.

I have no idea why he called. He said it was to simply see how I was getting on. He could have asked Julian, who is well tutored in telling his father nothing about me and only to use adjectives like *fine, satisfied and exuberant*. The last one Julian picked. I wanted *jolly*, but Julian said that should only be used in December or when describing a pirate's flag. Who knew a word could be dictated by your profession or the calendar? I didn't argue with him. The point was that he tells his father very little, and if he must talk about me, to keep it positive.

Derek had no news that I was interested in. He did tell me that he wanted to take the family to South Africa for Christmas. I asked him if he meant his old family or his new. He didn't answer that, but he did say that Olivia didn't want to go, so they'd decided to spend it at home this year. He seems to forget that Christmas with his old family was him not allowing Julian to open his presents until he was fed, showered and stinking of Drakkar Noir. Derek I mean, not Julian. Then, once all of the presents were opened, he used to go for a drive for a couple of hours. He would say it was because I would get too stressed if he got in the way in the kitchen. We now know he was spending time with his other family. I'm not bitter. It just irks me to know she was getting the Estée Lauder gift set while I was getting the Tefal pan set.

He then started talking about the wonderful Christmases he had here. By the time he had finished, I was beginning to think the Ghost of Christmas Past had visited him and shown him the wrong clip. He even went as far as to say my Christmas dinner was, and still is, the best he's ever tasted. He seems to have forgotten his incessant complaining of how long it took. I should have reminded him that for me, it was cooking, building Mousetrap and watching Julian do a puppet show while Derek fucked off to deliver the biggest goose he could find in Hampshire to his other family. But I didn't. I sat there and let him prattle on while I read this month's *Woman and Home* magazine and an interesting article about neck ageing.

Julian phoned to say that Derek called over at his house during the week. He'd brought them a card with a large cheque in it to help them set things up for the baby. I don't know how much he gave them, but when I spoke to Carrie, she said Julian was talking about putting it towards his child's education. She told him that the local school was fine and no child of hers was going to a private school. I think she's after a new fitted kitchen, truth be told.

Now, about us meeting. I think it's a splendid idea. Why don't you come here one weekend? I could show you some sights, not that there are many. Hampshire tends to be a summer county, I think. But the villages do some lovely light displays around this time of year. How about the end of the month? Would that be enough time for you to sort your dad out with Ruth? You can help me with finishing the nursery and finding some presents for the newborn. There's so much you can teach me with you having so many grandchildren.

Jane

x

To: jane-hubbard@skycorres.co.uk
From: daisyduke71@gomail.com
Date: Thursday, 5th November 21:53

Dear Jane

I have four grandchildren. I'm hardly Queen Victoria or an ambassador for Mothercare, but I'm sure between us, we can make your Zen room child-friendly with some cushion corners and find an age-appropriate rattle.

The fireworks are still going off around here. It's ten o'clock at night, for God's sake! I asked Dad if he wanted to see a firework display this evening, and he seemed up for it until I was helping him put his coat on. He asked where we were going, and when I told him, he said he didn't want to go. I was a bit disappointed, as I was going to drive over to the park by our Cheryl's and try and find them up there. I've got forty sparklers in my handbag now. I suppose they can play with them when they're next over. Our Bruno says he's too old, but he'll join in with the others as long as I let him be in charge of the lighter.

I have to say, not that I know him all that well, Derek seems to be acting strangely. It makes me wonder if there's trouble in paradise. Serves him right if there is. Just keep him at arm's length until you know what his game is. From my experience, if it doesn't involve women, then it will involve money, and you don't need to get involved with either. Anyway, I need to go. I can hear Dad swearing.

Lots of love

Daisy

xxx

To: jane-hubbard@skycorres.co.uk
From: daisyduke71@gomail.com
Date: Thursday, 5th November 23:10

Dear Jane

Sorry, my last email was cut short. I had to see to Dad. He could hear the fireworks going off and thought the Argentinians had invaded. I told him the conflict was finished, but he didn't believe me. Then I had to tell him that they'd left, as there was nothing for them to pillage from Chorley. He agreed and went back to bed.

Can you believe that? Still setting off fireworks at this time of night!

Lots of love

Daisy

xxx

To: daisyduke71@gomail.com
From: jane-hubbard@skycorres.co.uk
Date: **Friday, 6th November 10:30**

Dear Daisy

I hope you managed to get some sleep last night and the fireworks eventually subsided. Any celebrations here seemed to have concluded by nine p.m.

Julian called by this morning, as he's off work today. He and Carrie were going shopping to buy some baby items. I suspect they were using his father's money. I doubt the cheque has even cleared yet. Julian's always been the same. When he was young, most children would buy footballs or new pencil cases for school with their pocket money. Not Julian. He'd buy touch-up paint for his dummies and try to expand his teacup collection. At one point, he had enough cups to furnish an Intercity buffet car. The thing was, he never used them. They would languish in my cupboards while I rooted around, trying to find space for my Rick Stein cookbooks and Cath Kidston tea towels. He eventually took them to a local antique dealer, who laughed him out of the shop. So he ended up selling them at a car boot sale and managed to raise nearly £15 for his 'Travel the World' fund. The last I heard about that fund, it was still in his piggy bank and he'd amassed a fortune to get him as far as Hemel Hempstead. I've come to realise that my son is a snob. I have no idea where he gets it from.

I have to go to a church meeting later. We need to discuss upcoming events. Most of them are Christmas-related.

I've decided not to be a Buddhist, as I'm hoping to be the contact for the schools this year. There are two in the area that usually have their Christmas carol service with us. They're very easy to organise, plus, I know the school secretaries, so that helps. I have to say that if Floella gets the job, I shall be leaving the volunteer committee. She gets all the best jobs while the rest of us are cleaning or counting hymn books. You would not believe how many get stolen! I can't understand it. All Dominic ever sings is 'Morning Has Broken' and 'Amazing Grace'. I often wonder if a rogue choir is meeting in the village somewhere, clutching their stolen hymn books and feeling rebellious as they sing 'All Things Bright and Beautiful'.

Let me know as soon as you can about your visit.

Jane

x

To: jane-hubbard@skycorres.co.uk
From: daisyduke71@gomail.com
Date: Monday, 9ᵗʰ November 16:13

Dear Jane

I have just come off the phone to my sister, Ruth. After a very long conversation about who was the best daughter, I finally got her to agree to look after Dad for the weekend I come to you. She was arguing with me, saying he's only been with me five minutes and now I need a holiday to get over it. I ended up agreeing, saying she was made of sterner stuff than me, and that's why our parents favoured her. She seemed surprised by this, and so was I when it came out of my mouth. But at the time, I would have said anything, as Dad was trying to put a gas flame under the electric kettle.

She's agreed to stay here with him, as that's the easiest option. When I asked her whether Colin was joining her, she said she doubted it, as he had Amazon Prime installed recently and had a lot of catching up to do with Jeremy Clarkson. She also said she wouldn't mind having a bed all to herself for a couple of nights. So how about I come down next Friday? Let me know if this is okay.

Lots of love

Daisy

xxx

To: daisyduke71@gomail.com
From: jane-hubbard@skycorres.co.uk
Date: Wednesday, 11th November 18:22

Dear Daisy

Next Friday is perfect. I'll book us in a restaurant on the Saturday, and we can eat at home on the Friday, as you'll undoubtedly be shattered after the journey. I'll get a few bottles of Prosecco in, and I'll find all the music we used to dance to on the ship. However, we may have to push the sofa back for the 'Time Warp'. Let's see how we feel on the night. We can go to Southampton and do some Christmas shopping, or we can even jump on the train and head to London for the day. It's only a couple of hours to Waterloo.

Oh, I'm so excited.

Jane

x

To: jane-hubbard@skycorres.co.uk
From: daisyduke71@gomail.com
Date: Saturday, 14th November 09:47

Dear Jane

I've managed to sort everything with my sister Ruth and have started cooking some meals for her and Dad and popping them in the freezer. I'm trying to make things as easy for her as I possibly can, so if I ever need another favour in future, she won't mind so much. Our Cheryl wasn't happy, as it's Kelvin's brother's birthday on the Saturday that I'm with you. She said she wanted me to babysit the kids while she went out with them all to Nando's. She'd even bought a new halter-neck dress for the occasion. I told her that I'd struggle having the kids anyway, and she needed to realise this before she started buying new clothes. She got in a huff and asked does she need to check in with me every time she sees a new pair of shoes in case I want to abandon her and the grandkids again? I told her to grow up, find the receipt for the dress and ask Kelvin to bring her a chicken wrap back. I've not heard from her since. I suspect she's trying to convince Jade to have them.

I've not said anything to Dad about Ruth coming over. Sometimes when she visits, he doesn't know who she is. When she turned up the other day, he asked her if she was the neighbour from next door and if she could tell her kids to knock off the blaring records; there was only so much Duran Duran he could take. She apologised and helped him settle while he watched *Lovejoy*, and I made him a spam

sandwich. He has these outbursts, but fortunately, they don't last long.

Do I need to bring anything up with me? Do I tempt the gods if I bring my own pillow? Sorry, I couldn't resist. No, seriously, let me know if there's anything you'd like me to bring. It's been a long time since I was down south. James and I used to like going to Cornwall, as you know, but I've never been in your area. I hear the New Forest is beautiful. Maybe we could take a run out, and you can show me the ponies.

Lots of love

Daisy

xxx

To: jane-hubbard@skycorres.co.uk
From: daisyduke71@gomail.com
Date: Thursday, 19th November 10:18

Dear Jane

It was lovely chatting yesterday on the phone and sorting out all of the arrangements. Well, I'm all packed and ready to go. I know I'm not leaving until tomorrow, but I had to sneak a lot of stuff to the car. If Dad saw me loading the boot up in one go, he'd think he was going somewhere too or start having a fit about me taking him to the home.

Our Cheryl was over during the week. She carried on like nothing had been said. I told her Aunty Ruth was coming to look after Grandad. I watched her face, and I suspect she might have wanted to use the house to throw a party for Kelvin's brother. After having a nose in the freezer, she walked out, in a huff, of course, with one of Ruth's lasagnes. I shouted after her, saying that I was sure Kelvin would enjoy it more than the fish pie that was in there, seeing as he's still vegetarian.

I've given our Ruth the heads-up about Cheryl and not to be taken in by any sob story. She said that living with Colin all these years had given her the natural ability to know bullshit as soon as the handbrake was off. So I have no worries how she'll deal with all of the family in my absence. She might put up with a lot of crap in her life, but she's more clued up and far more resilient than me. She knows her life isn't perfect and says, "Show me someone with a perfect life, and I'll bet they have a drinking problem,

cook on an Aga and talk too much about their wellies."
I know a few of them.

Ruth says she knows Colin is a lazy oaf, but at least she
makes no pretence about him. Cheryl could do with opening
her eyes to Kelvin and seeing his faults. If she did, then she
could change him or get rid of him, but for a young girl to
be blind to it is a crying shame. I just wish she could see that
Kelvin needs a job, a purpose and a bar of Imperial Leather.

Anyway, I should be with you around three. I'll see you
tomorrow.

Lots of love

Daisy

xxx

To: jane-hubbard@skycorres.co.uk
From: daisyduke71@gomail.com
Date: Sunday, 22nd November 20:58

Dear Jane

Well, I'm home at last. I hope you got my text. I'm about to go to bed, but I just wanted to thank you for such a lovely weekend. I know you felt a little awkward when Dominic turned up out of the blue, but to be honest, I really liked him. He clearly thinks a lot of you. Yes, I know he's a vicar, but what's wrong with that? At least he has a job and is doing something he clearly enjoys. I found him very entertaining. Especially when he told us the story of opening the church hall for the homeless for the night, and they all ended up staying for over three months. It's such a shame the archdeacon couldn't see what a marvellous thing it was and ended up shutting it down. There was me thinking the church was full of Christians. Yes, I agree he might have been a little enthusiastic at the beginning, but he's obviously managed to quell his desire, or you haven't worn the apron in a while.

I've put all my Christmas shopping in the ottoman at the end of my bed. I don't think the grandkids know that it opens. They just sit on it and tell me all their tales. I miss that. I still have a lot more to buy, including Dad's. I need to have my thinking hat on about that. What on earth can I buy a man whose head is stuck in the eighties and still thinks that Ceefax is the eighth wonder of the world? He used to like painting and making things. I might see if I can get him something like that.

I know you know what you have from me. I'm so glad I spotted that Estée Lauder gift set. Who needs a man? Not us. I bet Olivia is getting the pans now, seeing as she can't cook a Christmas dinner as well as her predecessor. But even though you have a present, I will still send a little something over. I can hear you now shouting "No!" but believe me when I say it's just a little something, and the postage will probably cost more than the gift itself.

Our Ruth said everything was fine while I was away. Dad had a lucid moment on the Sunday morning and asked where I was and why Ruth was sleeping in my bed. She said he was worried for a moment that I'd taken ill. She was surprised at how long he was with her and asked if the grandkids had come and if they understood what was happening. But by the time she finished telling him they were fine and still loved him, he was asking for Ovaltine and wanted it made with real milk, not Marvel. He hasn't had Ovaltine since Mum died, and she used to make it with Marvel because he didn't know the difference. It seems he did and never said.

She said if I ever wanted to go on holiday again, then she would be more than happy to stay and that she had a lovely time. I'm not surprised! She didn't have to cook or do laundry, and it looks like my Bayliss and Harding bath set has taken a battering in my absence. How the hell she had time for a bath, I don't know. After I've done a full day's work, made the dinner, looked after Dad, done the laundry and put him to bed, the most I can manage is to give my face a lick with a tissue and remember to put my phone on charge. I can't remember the last time I had a bath.

About Christmas, remember what I said? You're very welcome to come here for Christmas Day if you don't think you'll be spending it with Julian and Carrie. I'm sure all will be well.

Again, thank you for a lovely visit, and it's no wonder you made such a fuss of your Dunnypillows. I had one of the best sleeps ever last night. But that could have been on account of us drinking five bottles of Prosecco and dancing to Bucks Fizz three times in succession. I hope you managed to fix the seam on your skirt!

Lots of love

Daisy

xxx

To: daisyduke71@gomail.com
From: jane-hubbard@skycorres.co.uk
Date: Tuesday, 24th November 22:01

Dear Daisy

I'm so glad you enjoyed your visit. You were a much better house guest than I was…

Dominic came over not long after you left and said he was sorry that he didn't have a chance to say goodbye. He also found you very entertaining and said your impression of Keith Lemon was quite remarkable. I said I must've missed that, as I couldn't recall you doing impressions. He seemed to think you'd kept it up for most of his visit. I must admit the time he was here showed a side to him that I'd not seen before. Even when he came after you'd left, he made no advance and simply said goodbye when he left the house. Maybe he's gone off me.

I received a text from Derek asking if I had a nice time with my friend. He kept overusing the word 'friend', which made me think he didn't know you were a woman. I've only told Julian that I had a friend over for the weekend, and because he didn't ask who it was, I didn't say. He must've gone back to his father and told him, and they've jumped to the wrong conclusion. I've no intention of correcting him. If he thinks I'm having wild sex instead of decorating the nursery, then I'm in no rush to correct him.

By the way, thank you for all your marvellous tips on what to buy for the baby. Who knew puppy pads could have so many uses? And I must tell Carrie the story of you putting a picture of a potato on the pinboard and telling the children it was a picture of their sister because she wouldn't wash properly or brush her teeth. I feel I'm now ready to be a lone grandmother, knowing you have so much experience to impart.

To get back to Derek, I said I had a wonderful time and no doubt I would be seeing my friend soon, as I had a lot of time and love for them. I do wonder how that landed. I'll probably never know.

I must go. I need to get to sleep and get up early to collect the car seat from John Lewis. I know you said it's a little early to buy one for when the child is over eleven years of age, but it won't take up any room in the garage, and it's one less thing to think about.

Jane

x

To: jane-hubbard@skycorres.co.uk
From: daisyduke71@gomail.com
Date: Tuesday, 1st December 21:01

Dear Jane

I've just had our Cheryl round moaning about her life, saying all she ever does is look after kids and wash Kelvin's socks. I'm not sure she does the latter particularly well, but she moaned incessantly. Even Dad rolled his eyes at one point, even though he thought she was the Avon lady and had come to collect the catalogue. She went on to say how she's not appreciated and never goes out anymore (even though she managed to get Jade to babysit the other day) and how she's the only person she knows who has four kids.

I told her that I would contact Carol Vorderman and make sure she was included in the line-up for the next Pride of Britain Awards. She started shouting, saying I wasn't taking her situation seriously, and I said I understood it more than she ever understood contraception. She left screaming that I would probably have been happier with her going to a backstreet abortionist and her bleeding to death in a back alley somewhere. I told her to go home and Google the NHS, and while she had the computer open, to ask Google how often to clean the grill. Last time I went there, I made the kids' cheese on toast, and the neighbour nearly called the fire brigade due to the plumes of smoke billowing out of the back door. When they finished eating, I thought the kids were going to start singing 'Chim Chim Cher-ee', their faces were that sooty! I do hope your Carrie keeps house better than our Cheryl. I'm sure she will. I'm sure your

Carrie knows that Matey is not a multipurpose cleaner and *The Chase* is not an educational programme.

Sorry for ranting, but just when I think I've got everything on an even keel, someone throws a spanner in the works. If it's not Cheryl, then it's Dad. The other day, I was upstairs changing his bed and noticed a draught. When I went to investigate, he was wandering down the street, trying to figure out how many tables we'd need for the street party. When I asked who the street party was for, he said Charles and Diana's wedding. I didn't have the heart to tell him she was gone and he'd married someone else. I mean, how can you explain to someone that a man married Camilla after Diana? I told him that Mrs Pemberton had it all in hand, and I would make sure that she'd ordered the two hundred tables he felt were needed for our small cul-de-sac. I'm going to have to look at the locks on the doors.

Sorry again for moaning. I'm just finding it all a bit hard lately. It won't be long before I have a few days off from work, and then I can look at how I can make things a little easier around here. Hopefully, the incessant growl of Slade in every shop I go into lately will inject some Christmas spirit.

Love

Daisy

xxx

To: daisyduke71@gomail.com
From: jane-hubbard@skycorres.co.uk
Date: Friday, 4th December 12:17

Dear Daisy

I'm a grandmother! Carrie had the baby yesterday. They've called her Myla, and she weighs seven pounds and five ounces. She has a headful of dark hair and the most perfect eyebrows I've ever seen. Carrie ended up having a home birth simply because labour accelerated so quickly. The ambulance man walked into the room just as I pulled Myla out. Julian missed the actual birth, as he insisted the baby was to be born underwater. While he was running the bath, he didn't hear the ambulance people arrive. It was only when he came in to see if the baby would be okay with a splash of Molton Brown in the water that he realised his daughter had already arrived.

When I passed his daughter over to him, it was the only time I'd seen Julian stunned and lost for words. Carrie was incredible. I'm not sure I could've given birth in front of Derek's mother. She had unfathomable depths of prudishness. I once wore a three-inch heel in the local Beefeater restaurant and she accused me of being promiscuous. She also told me that anyone who thinks oral sex is an obligatory part of marriage needs to stop watching Channel Four. Derek was terrified of her. Thinking about it now, he may have only married me so he could get away from her.

Anyway, I've attached a couple of photos of the baby. Excuse the startled expression on Julian's face. I'm not sure if that was because he'd just become a father or if the flash on the phone was a little blinding. They took Carrie to hospital to check her and Myla over, and when I called Julian earlier, he said that they could come home later today and could I make sure that I was there when they got home? I asked him if he was asking his father to come too, but he recalled his father saying that they were taking Ben to Alton Towers for his birthday and were coming home later tonight. It seems that Ben and Myla share the same birthday. It's bizarre to think Myla has a half-uncle who's only eight years old. And there was Derek's mother saying *I* was promiscuous.

I must go and get ready to welcome Myla home. I wanted you to be the first to know. You are very precious to me. As soon as we can, you must meet Myla. I know you will love her.

Jane

x

To: jane-hubbard@skycorres.co.uk
From: daisyduke71@gomail.com
Date: Friday, 4th December 20:29

Dear Jane

Congratulations!! Wow! Wow! Wow! And you delivered her on your own. Don't you ever tell me that you are incapable of anything ever again. You are a superwoman, and I am proud to call you my friend. I cannot wait to meet her. We'll have to sort something out in the New Year when I know when Ruth can sit with Dad. I have a gift here that I'll send to yours, and you can give it to them the next time you see them.

You must tell me how today went. Was it lovely to welcome her home? I know she was born there, but even still, it all seems a bit more official when they come home from the hospital. I must admit when I brought our Cheryl home, most of my family was there to welcome her, and my dad had made a huge hotpot for everyone. I only have to smell it now, and I can hear our Cheryl crying for her bottle. She's still the same, only now she cries for Polski vodka. Send more photos. I want to see her with you!

Lots of love

Daisy

xxx

To: daisyduke71@gomail.com
From: jane-hubbard@skycorres.co.uk
Date: Friday, 11th December 12:17

Dear Daisy

Sorry, it's been a whole week since I spoke to you, but I'm sure you understand. Well, as I said, Myla and Carrie came home last week. Only Julian, Derek, Carrie's friend Celia from the shop, and I were there to welcome her home. I asked Julian where all of Carrie's friends were, and he said she didn't have a wide circle of friends. It seems her mother told her not to mix with people who ate meat, shopped in supermarkets or owned a television as it was cancer for the intellect. I never knew this about Carrie. She must've been very lonely as a child, even if her mother did think that carving friends out of Maris Piper potatoes and painting them pink would satisfy a child who just wanted Malibu Barbie.

I knew Carrie had a sheltered upbringing, but I had no idea to what extent. While Julian said he has the life task of normalising her, I do worry that some of these experiences may rub off on Myla. I couldn't bear to walk in and see my granddaughter trying to put a parsnip in a pair of hot pants and a matching boob tube. Hopefully, I'll have enough influence on the whole family to ensure that vegetables are for the oven and that television is very educational. Wasn't it David Attenborough who discovered plastic was killing the planet and told everyone to invent electric cars? My rubbish is filed better than my household accounts, and I have David

to thank for that and Brabantia for their wide selection
of bins.

As I said, Derek was at the house to welcome Myla home.
There was no sign of Olivia or Ben. When I asked where
they were, he mumbled something about Ben having the
sniffles, and he and Julian agreed that it would be best if
they stayed at home. They were also expecting a delivery, so
someone had to be there, as Lena, the nanny, returned to
Warsaw. I couldn't get to the bottom of this and couldn't tell
if she was returning or had actually left them. He quickly
changed the subject and asked if I'd seen my friend lately.
When I said I was in constant contact with my friend, he
looked a little taken aback. He started asking whether my
friend was special. I told him they were a little more special
than the gentleman I'd spent the weekend in London with
and a lot more than the man who constantly knocks on my
door looking for more than a rummage in my biscuit tin.
He said I've changed, and he's not sure if it's for the better.
I told him that his opinion of me not only doesn't matter but
is of no interest to anyone except himself. He sulked most of
the time we were there.

Celia seemed a strange sort. She works with Carrie in the
car accessory shop, and I'm sure her knowledge of the V8
engine could only be rivalled by the presenters of *Top Gear*.
Julian had to tell her to change the subject, as he felt the
conversation was unsuitable for a baby's homecoming.
She struggled to converse after that and only became
aminated when I told her I drove a Mercedes, and she
whispered that despite a rising difference of opinion, she felt
that German cars were superior to any others and enthused

so much I thought she might goosestep over to the small buffet I'd laid out.

Carrie is still a little awkward with the baby. I'm sure all new mothers are the same. I remember when Julian was born, I didn't know how to hold him properly. Derek's mother told me off as I was trying to sit him up on my knee as soon as he was born. I didn't know any different. I do wonder if that's why Julian found holding ventriloquist dummies natural.

I asked Julian if he'd managed to contact Carrie's mum, but he said they had no way of finding her, and Carrie could only hope that one day her mother would turn up after seeking her out instead. Carrie still works in the same shop as she did when her mother left, so it wouldn't be hard for her to find Carrie if she really wanted to. I would love to try and look for her, but I have no idea where to start or even if my efforts would be appreciated.

I stayed until Julian started making noises about everyone feeling a bit tired, so we all left at the same time. Derek looked like he wanted to say something as we all got into our cars, but I've no interest in anything that man has to say anymore. I'm so surprised at how quickly I've gotten over his duplicitous lifestyle and how little I want to interact with him. I thought I was desperately in love with the man, but now I'm not so sure. I no doubt loved him, but maybe that was because he provided for me and gave me Julian. Would I have felt the same degree of happiness if I was childless and living somewhere like Milton Keynes? There was no great passion between us. Maybe that was why he ran off into Olivia's arms. She looks the type to watch Channel Four.

The rest of the week has been me popping into Julian's every day. Believe me when I say this is Julian's neediness coming to the fore. I told him on Tuesday that I would see him towards the end of the week, and he nearly dropped to his knees, begging me to come back the following day. I said that he and Carrie needed to settle with Myla on their own, but he said I would always be part of their lives, so what difference did it make if I saw them every day, now or later? I was going to argue with him, but Carrie stepped in and said she found my help invaluable. It's nice to be wanted, I suppose.

Olivia sent a silver rattle engraved with Myla's name, weight and date of birth. Julian asked was the baby supposed to play with it? When I said it was an ornament and probably cost a lot of money, it took pride of place on one of the shelves in the nursery—the shelf is above the changing table. So every time I change the baby's nappy, I'm reminded that Olivia's probably never changed a nappy in her life; she passed all of that responsibility to skinny Lena.

Anyway, I must close. I'm exhausted. I don't know how you manage with four.

Jane

x

To: jane-hubbard@skycorres.co.uk
From: daisyduke71@gomail.com
Date: Saturday, 12th December 19:45

Dear Jane,

What a day! I've managed to do the rest of my Christmas shopping all in one go. I just made a list, went to the Trafford Centre and periodically ran to the car to fill the boot throughout the day. I don't have a lot of people to buy for, but our Cheryl still expects the tree to be half-hidden by her mountain of presents. I keep telling her she's not a child anymore, but then she pouts to prove me wrong. When will that girl ever grow up?

Our Bruno is mad about football, so I got him his team's home and away kits, plus everything in the shop that had the club's emblem on it. Beyoncé just wants more clothes for her dolls, so I bought her a few outfits for her favourite dolly, as well as a new pram, cot, bedding and a pretend baby monitor. The twins are at the age when they just want to make lots of noise. So I bought them a load of musical instruments. I know our Cheryl will go mad, but you have to nurture them at a young age. I keep telling her that years ago, if you had a family with more than three kids, it was expected that they would end up singing. The Bee Gees, The Corrs, Oasis—all family bands. She told me they were all shit. But I was quick to point out, shit or not, they were all rich. She's now got them trying to sing 'ABC' by the Jackson 5, but our Bruno asked whether they could sing something else because he's dyslexic. I don't expect to see them on any talent show, but I wouldn't tell them that. I just clap in all the right places to keep them happy for now.

I bought Dad the complete box sets for *Minder*, *The Professionals*, *The A-Team* and *Bergerac*. That should keep him happy for at least six months—as long as he remembers how to use the DVD player. I had to throw the VCR away last month when I caught him trying to toast a crumpet in it.

Me and my sister Ruth don't bother buying each other presents anymore. We just try and have a catch-up in January and make it a nice day out somewhere. Last year, we went to a castle and had a cream tea and some bubbles. It was such a lovely day. I was going to invite her over for lunch on Christmas Day, but she said Colin just wants it to be the two of them this year. I can't blame them; they've had Dad for the last decade, so it really is my turn to give them some peace. Not that I had it when they did have Dad. I always have Cheryl, Kelvin and the four kids, so this year will be no different. I just expect there to be a bit more arguing this year between Cheryl and her grandad. But we'll see.

I do miss the Christmases when James was alive and our Cheryl was little. It was just the three of us for a few years. When Mum was alive, she and Dad would have Christmas at Aunty Pauline's, and we'd all see other on Boxing Day with our Ruth. But when Mum died, well, they all kind of stopped. Such a shame, really. They were fun.

Not surprisingly, we spoiled our Cheryl. Whatever she wanted, she got, and I wonder why now she is the way she is. James and I constantly indulged her, and now she has a man who might not spoil her with material things, but to take on four kiddies that aren't his tells me he's generous in other ways, even though he gets on my nerves and forces me to breathe through my mouth.

Just thinking about it, our Cheryl's never had a Christmas without me. It's kind of expected that she and the kids come to me. Plus, she doesn't know how to peel potatoes, what turkey giblets are or that baked beans are not vegetables. I don't think she's ever cooked for them all to eat at the same time. She'll feed Bruno first because he only eats chicken nuggets, so she can get him fed while he does his homework. Beyoncé will eat with the twins, who are all partial to a Pot Noodle. Then Cheryl and Kelvin will get a takeaway once the kids are in bed. Is it any wonder that I insist they come to me once a week for their tea? They all think it's because I need to see them, which is true to a certain extent, but it's more to get some fresh food down them, including Kelvin. I gave him a roast dinner last month and served it with parsnips. After he asked what they were and me telling him, I heard him whisper to our Cheryl, "Why do she have to cook exotic food?" Even she rolled her eyes. Parsnips? Exotic? I'm making cannelloni next time he comes, which will undoubtedly blow his mind. The only pasta he's seen comes in hoops.

Well, I've got to go. Dad's been shouting me for fifteen minutes, wondering where the remote control is. I have to hide it, as he has the volume up so high that Mrs Pemberton complained that she found watching a film about Jesus Christ an upsetting experience, as she could hear through the wall Yosser Hughes from *Boys from the Blackstuff* shouting, 'Giz a job!' while Jesus was being nailed to the cross. So now I have to keep it low and put the subtitles on for him.

Speak soon.

Love Daisy

xxx

To: daisyduke71@gomail.com
From: jane-hubbard@skycorres.co.uk
Date: Saturday, 19th December 07:42

Dear Daisy

My apologies for the early email. I need your advice, as I'm feeling slightly confused. Dominic came over last night. He said he wanted to see if I would be available to help with the Christmas Eve service. It's always popular and the only time when we have people standing at the back except when *Songs of Praise* was filmed there. I didn't know half the faces that turned up for that. The man from the BBC said they have groupies that follow them around, hoping to be 'discovered' as they belt out 'How Great Thou Art'. Apparently, they had to ban one woman when they were in Middlesbrough when they caught her twerking to 'All Things Bright and Beautiful'.

Anyway, I said I would as long as I wasn't with Floella. He said she wouldn't be working in the church anymore, as she'd come to him and told him that her commitments to running her scented-candle empire had to take precedence. Her candle empire is a shop on the high street next to the French dining furniture shop. I think she thought that being next to a shop called Jambe de Sciure would make her sophisticated. She clearly didn't take French in school; if she had, she wouldn't have questioned why the butcher moved to Market Square.

Her range of candles totals four, and they all have pretentious names. One of them is called Whispering Wood. Tell me what that's supposed to smell like. It could be anything from a pine tree to a Swan Vesta match. She once asked me when I would pop into her shop. When I said when she's finished stocking it, she said that was the look she was going for. Clean and minimal. What's the point of having a shop if you're not going to stock it? It made me wonder—if I had taken up candle making, would I have a shop by now?

Anyway, Dominic said he was glad she wasn't involved anymore, as her help could sometimes be overwhelming. In my house, we call it bossy. So I'll be helping him on Christmas Eve instead of just attending the service. Do you think I should buy him a gift? I would feel strange seeing someone on Christmas Eve and not give them something, but I think that might give him the wrong impression. Then I thought would it be so bad if he made another move? He was talking about another parishioner called Dee a lot. She moved here from Scunthorpe, and Dominic finds her very amusing—his opinion, not mine. He continued to bring her up as we talked about the Nativity, how many hymn books we would need and the latest *Radio Times*. I might go as far as to say he is obsessed.

So, I don't know if I'm miffed at the thought of me not being on his radar anymore or the fact that someone else is. I know! I'm a hypocrite! It wasn't that long ago I was chasing him out of the house, cursing him because he'd depleted my garibaldis. I'm being horribly green, aren't I?

In other news, Julian and Carrie finally managed Myla on their own one day. I told them I had a cold (lie), so I couldn't see them. Later, Julian called and was very pleased that they had coped with the day fairly admirably. I said that was just as well, as he had roughly another seven thousand to complete. After a moment's silence, he asked if my cold had cleared up. I told him I hoped it was a twenty-four-hour cold (is there such a thing?), but I still felt quite unwell and didn't want to pass it on to any of them, especially Carrie. He seemed surprised by this and asked why not the baby? I pointed out that if a baby is sick, it has its parents to nurse it, but if a parent gets sick, they still have to look after the baby. It will take a while, but hopefully, Julian will soon see that to cope, he and Carrie will be buying a lot more wine. By the time Julian was ten, I could have qualified as a sommelier. Mind you, I'm still not sure what is best with fish as opposed to duck, but I can tell you what is best for tantrums as opposed to general cheekiness.

I asked him if his father had visited, but he said no, which means that Olivia has still not met the baby. While she may not be related to Myla, her son is. Maybe she has so much family of her own, she doesn't feel the need to see what little we have. Derek was an only child, and so was I. Then with Julian also being an only child, any extended family was non-existent. Julian has never had an aunt, uncle or cousin. We did discuss once, when Julian was about five, about having another baby, but then Derek became distracted with the electric tin opener that became wedged stuck in a can of John West mandarin orange segments and the subject was never raised again.

Derek has texted twice in the last week. That's two times more than he did in the last year of our marriage. One was to ask me if I could recall what we had to eat at a lovely restaurant in Torquay when we were first married, and the other enquired if I would be seeing Myla over the weekend or seeing my friend. The first, I didn't know, and the second I said both. Both of these are a lie. We had lobster in the first, which I'm sure he knew. It was the only time we ever had lobster, as Derek found it uncomfortable picking one out. He said it was barbaric to pick your food before you ate it while he selected his sides from the extensive menu. Even the waiter shook his head.

Anyway, I must go and deliver my Christmas cards and maybe find a gift for Dominic.

Jane

x

To: jane-hubbard@skycorres.co.uk
From: daisyduke71@gomail.com
Date: Saturday, 26th December 21:31

Dear Jane,

Sorry I didn't call you back yesterday. As you can imagine, I was up to my eyes with Cheryl, Dad and all the grandkids. Even Mrs Pemberton popped in and ended up staying for two hours, as she and Dad got into a conversation about the miners' strike and Arthur Scargill. It was good to see Dad animated and passionate about something. Mrs Pemberton is such an intelligent woman, so she and Dad are on the same level. I didn't like to tell her that he thinks the strike only started last month. I think she would still be sitting on my settee now, only for her son picking her up and taking her over to their house for her Christmas lunch.

Dad was disappointed when she left. He tried to engage with Kelvin about it, who said that the strike had no effect on him, as when he grew up, they only had an electric three-bar fire anyway. I think if Dad had a gun, he would have shot him for his sheer stupidity. Dad might have dementia, but he's not lost his intelligence. He rolled his eyes at him all through dinner and dessert, which upset me, as I'd trudged over half the North West trying to find hundreds and thousands for the trifle that he shovelled into his angry mouth.

The kids enjoyed their day. They all got ruined as usual, but that's what it's all about. Our Cheryl wasn't happy, though. I think she thought that Kelvin might have popped the question and given her an engagement ring. He bought her a set of pans and some underwear that looked like it could cut cheese and a small piece at that. I think that will be going back.

She bought me a lovely scarf and some sleeping bags to keep in mine for the kids, as half the beds have gone now. She's determined to have me back on board as chief babysitter. It's not happening, but I'll keep the sleeping bags for when they come over for the day and they want to build dens. Dad likes doing that with them. Last time, he got hot and took his shirt off, and the kids saw his chickenpox scars all over his back. When Sharpay asked where they'd come from, he said they were from arrows when he fought the Indians with Custer in 1876. The younger kids didn't bat an eyelid, but our Bruno gave him a funny look. A wink from Dad soon had him joining in with fighting an imaginary Indian called Big Baggy Y-fronts.

Kelvin took the kids home last night, but our Cheryl stayed, as she'd drunk a whole bottle of port, started on the advocaat, threw up and went into a coma on the couch. I said to leave her and that I would run her home today. I wanted her to stay as I could get no sense out of her. When she got drunk, she only went on one of those dating websites and put my details in. Well, the next thing you know, my phone was dinging so much I thought I was having an attack of tinnitus. I told her this morning to get the thing off, but she started looking at who was sending the messages. Some, I have to say, were that bad I was looking for the bolts, and they're so forward in their messages. My head was spinning with it all. I wasn't sure what to read or what buttons to press—like the self-serve ticket machine at a London Underground station. Chaos!

She kept insisting we should have a look. I told her it always seems innocent initially, and they always say they want to take it slow. Then before you know it, you've been wined and dined in Miller and Carter, and they think that gives them the right to come back to your house, get their leg over and start singing 'Lady Marmalade' while they're in your shower getting pubes in your bar of Shield.

Anyway, after all that, she ignored me, and to cut a long story short, I've got a date tomorrow with a man called Jeff. He's from Liverpool, but he says he will drive over and we can go for a meal as he knows a nice place near Duxbury Woods. Our Cheryl wasn't keen on the idea of meeting near the woods in case he was a serial killer. But when I told her someone died when they got hit over the head with a ukulele as they walked out of Greggs in the middle of Chorley, she realised that you could pop your clogs anywhere.

So Jeff is fifty-eight, lives on his own, divorced, and has two kids at university. He said he's an accountant and works for himself. Our Ruth is coming over to keep an eye on Dad for a couple of hours. I hope he's better than the last one. I don't think I could cope with the sight of another man going through my Andrex looking like a maypole dancer.

I'll email you later in the week and let you know how it all went.

Love Daisy

xxx

To: daisyduke71@gomail.com
From: jane-hubbard@skycorres.co.uk
Date: Sunday, 27th December 11:11

Dear Daisy

First, can I say good luck with your date? I cannot wait to hear all about Jeff. I've never met a person from Liverpool before. I've only seen them on television and get the impression that they could be fun, but I'm not sure I would be able to understand them. I had to put the subtitles on when I watched *Brookside* years ago; even then, I still struggled with their dialect. Why do they say 'sound' at the end of some conversations?

My Christmas was a lot quieter than yours. I only had Julian, Carrie and Myla over for lunch. They wanted to shoot back, as Derek had promised them he would pop in with their gifts. I must tell you, though, that Derek was texting me all morning, still reminiscing about Christmases past like a Dickensian ghost. He then suggested that he come over to my house and that he could see Julian here. I told him that was out of the question and that if he wanted to see his son, he should sort it out with him direct. Then he sent a strange text saying it wasn't just Julian he wanted to see. I completely ignored that, sent Julian on his way once Myla had her feed and then texted him back to say they were on their way home. Carrie texted me at half ten last night to say they were still waiting. What a swine! He was undoubtedly distracted by Olivia swanning around in her latest diamond necklace. I don't know if he bought her a necklace, but she strikes me as someone who would need a new piece of jewellery to show off while she tells the caterers how many people will be coming for Christmas lunch.

Enough about them. I do have some news of my own. As you know, I offered my services to the church on Christmas Eve and finally met Dee. Well, I don't mind telling you that I see her as no threat. She turned up in a pair of dungarees that she teamed up with slingbacks. She said she wanted to get dressed up, seeing as it was Christmas Eve, and hoped Dominic appreciated the effort. If she was aiming for the look of a TV children's presenter who'd lost a decent pair of shoes, she nailed it as far as I'm concerned. I wore a simple green dress from Coast, and when Dominic said how nice I looked, she pointed out her footwear to him, waiting for a similar compliment. When she asked if he liked them, he simply said they looked as comfortable as her outfit. She seemed happy with this and click-clacked her way around the pews, distributing the hymn books.

The service went well, and the attendance was high. I helped later with tea and mince pies in the church hall, and when Dominic told Dee to go home as he and I would be clearing up, I got the impression he wanted me on my own. Sure enough, once the last cup was put away, he produced a gift for me. My relief in buying him a gift was short-lived when I opened the most exquisite jewellery box. He said he found it in an antique shop and thought I would like it. He said I struck him as someone who had nice jewellery and deserved a lovely box to put it all in. I didn't have the heart to tell him that most of what I have is tat from Ratners, and no doubt Olivia had all the decent stuff. But to be honest, it's simply a beautiful box to look at, even if it is empty.

I gave him a leather bookmark that I had embossed with the quote, 'What you become is your gift to God'. I picked one that was extra-long so he could use it with the large bible in the church. He seemed quite choked when he looked at it. While not as generous as his gift to me, I think he was genuinely touched by it.

Anyway, he walked me out to the car park, where we shared a Christmas kiss. Nothing desperately passionate, but I have to say that it was one of the sweetest kisses I've ever had. I asked him where was the flirty vicar who confessed his feelings to me not so long ago. He apologised again and said that maybe the garibaldis had suppressed his passion, but he still often thought of me in my Carmen Miranda outfit.

He texted me yesterday and wished me Happy Christmas, but I've not heard from him since. I hope he's just busy and not ignoring me. It would be just my luck that the minute I let my guard down, he'll find fun with Dee and her multi-pocketed dungarees.

Let me know how your date goes.

Jane

x

To: daisyduke71@gomail.com
From: jane-hubbard@skycorres.co.uk
Date: Sunday, 27th December 22:52

Dear Daisy

I was going to call you, but then I remembered you're on your date with Jeff, and I wondered if I should disturb you, as I have an emergency.

Olivia turned up at the house today with Ben and a *lot* of luggage! She's left Derek. She was begging to come in as she needed advice and had just checked out of the local Travelodge where she spent Christmas. She could see I was shocked, but what could I do when someone has a seven-year-old in tow?

She's still here. Cutting a very long story short, she said things were never the same once she gave birth to Ben. She said she started to see a side to him that she didn't particularly like, and apparently, she never asked him to leave me. He turned up on the doorstep one day and said that he had left me and was moving in with her. As he was paying the mortgage and her bills, she felt she had no choice but to let him in. She apologised for contributing to the breakdown of our marriage, but he gave her the impression that we were more or less separated, and he was quite certain that I had another man. So she saw no reason not to pursue her affair with a man who was more or less single. She said it was only when she became pregnant that she realised he wanted his bread buttered on both sides, and he was scared of the financial implications of splitting up. Who said romance was dead?

I asked her why she had come to me out of all the people in the world she could have asked for help. She said her parents lived in Jersey, and she wasn't that close to them anymore. She also said that the few friends she'd made when she moved to the area had dropped her when they heard she'd broken up a marriage. In the end, her only friend was Lena, the nanny, who left because Derek kept haggling with her over her wages. Olivia hadn't known that until she was contacted for a reference from a pet food manufacturer when Lena applied for a job there as a taster.

Olivia can't understand why Derek's so mean with his money. As far as she's concerned, the company's doing well. So anyway, I was the only other person she knew. What could I say?

That now tells me why Derek has been sniffing around so much lately and why he wanted to come over on Christmas Day. He was obviously on his own, as I asked Olivia when she'd heard from him last. She said it was Christmas Eve, and even then, it was to talk to Ben briefly. I didn't have the heart to tell her that he was angling for an invite from me.

I've made a bed up for her and Ben in the spare room with the blow-up mattress. She's left her luggage in the car, as she plans to leave tomorrow. When I asked her where she was going to go, she said she had no idea. I encouraged her to go back to the house and tell Derek to leave, but she said that house never felt like her home. It's all in Derek's name, and the fact that he watched her leave tells her he won't be quick to see her back in.

So there was me thinking she was dripping in diamonds like Elizabeth Taylor, and all the while, she was in a dingy hotel eating McDonald's on the bed. Regardless of how I feel about her, which I must admit I'm a little confused about now, I wouldn't wish that on anyone.

Do you think I did the right thing letting her stay? Do you think I should tell Derek? Or even Julian, for that matter? I feel like I'm harbouring a fugitive.

Please tell me what to do!

Jane

x

To: jane-hubbard@skycorres.co.uk
From: daisyduke71@gomail.com
Date: **Monday, 28th December 8:50**

Dear Jane,

I just logged on now for work and saw your email! I had to read it three times to make sure that I understood it right.

I'll start by saying your heart is bigger than her balls, and that's saying something. Of all the doors to knock on, she knocked on yours. How has she explained you to Ben? That poor thing. You must tell Julian or Carrie, at least. If this gets out, Derek will no doubt blame you, or worse, Julian will. Does she have any money? Does this mean she'll lose her job as well? All that on top of losing the nanny to the Pedigree Chum factory. She must be on the verge of a nervous breakdown.

You must tell someone she is there. This could all blow up in your face.

Love

Daisy

xxx

To: daisyduke71@gomail.com
From: jane-hubbard@skycorres.co.uk
Date: Monday, 28th December 23:48

Dear Daisy

She's still here. I didn't have the heart to tell her to leave, especially with Ben. He really is a sweet boy. He reminds me a little of Julian when he was younger, except Julian was a lot more mature for his age. There were not many seven-year-olds who could challenge a doctor on his qualifications when he was diagnosed with a verruca. At the very least, Julian felt he should be referred to an oncologist or a dermatologist. We were sent away with a prescription for Bazuka That Verruca and a nasty look from Dr Simone. I can't imagine Ben doing that.

Olivia was very appreciative of me letting her stay another night. She called her mother and told her the whole story, but by all accounts, there was not much sympathy coming from Jersey, and her father said he would put some money into an account for her to tide her over. I'm not sure how much he sent, but it can't be much, as she asked if I would look after Ben tomorrow while she went out to look for a job. I've told her that it's not fair that she should lose her job as well as her home. Derek is the bastard here. He still hasn't checked that they're okay.

I know you say I should contact him, but I'm not sure how that will help. I did think of calling Julian, but he can barely cope with his own family, never mind a secret one that he only found out about recently. He's in a panic because I put

165

a little announcement in the local paper about Myla's birth. He's worried that Carrie's mother may see it and turn up on their doorstep. I told him I wasn't sure that the *Lymington News* was delivered as far as the South of France, and even if it was, her mother was probably brain-addled from eating Quorn and sniffing patchouli the last fifteen years.

I've told Olivia she can stay until she gets herself sorted. As soon as I said it, you could see her visibly relax. Her face softened, and she looked pretty. I could see why Derek left me, and I wanted to slap her. How bad is that? But then she began to tell me I was the kindest person she had ever known and she couldn't understand why anyone would leave me, especially for her. That was when I realised that the girl's self-esteem was as low as her impeccable shoes. It seems Derek has chipped away at her over the years. I gave her a hug and said if I could get over Derek, then she could too. She has Ben and me to help her. I had no one and revealed to her that I would often talk to Julian's dummy, Thin Lizzy.

So that's the state of affairs today. I'll update you know tomorrow.

Jane

x

To: jane-hubbard@skycorres.co.uk
From: daisyduke71@gomail.com
Date: **Thursday, 31st December 17:41**

Dear Jane,

I thought I would email you before I go out for New Year.
I expected to have heard from you by now about how things
are going. I hope they're all okay. Just drop me a quick line.
I have visions of Derek turning into Ted Bundy, standing
over you, Olivia and Ben while Julian's blood-spattered
dummies look on with relish.

I'm going to a party up the road in one of the neighbour's
houses, and I've invited Jeff along. Our date went very well
the other night. He is very funny and reminds me a little
of Paul Hollywood, except he has brown eyes and can't
bake. He revealed that he is also an artist, and from what
I can see on Google, he's quite successful and really rather
good. Some of his work is hanging in some of the upmarket
restaurants in the city. He tends to do the human form more
than anything, and when I looked him up, you could tell
that a particular woman has been used in a lot of his work.
It turns out it's his ex-wife. She looks beautiful, but he said
she didn't age well. He didn't talk about her too much.

I hope you have something fun planned for this evening
and haven't had to cancel anything because Olivia is there.
I'll try and call you at midnight.

Love

Daisy

xxx

To: daisyduke71@gomail.com
From: jane-hubbard@skycorres.co.uk
Date: Friday, 1st January 12:33

Dear Daisy

Happy New Year! Sorry I missed your call last night. I went to bed not long after midnight. Olivia and I stayed up and watched the fireworks being set off in the garden around the back. He always puts on a good display. Apparently, he was in jail for arson a couple of years back, and that's how he can put on a bit of a show. Olivia said she wished Ben had seen them as he would have loved them. When I asked her if she was comfortable knowing an ex-felon lived only a few hundred yards away, she revealed that her uncle was a bank robber and died after fleeing to Spain. Apparently, the taxi that was running him from the airport to his new villa blew a tyre and fell down a ravine killing him and the taxi driver. She said her family never liked him anyway, and even though she was young when he died, she still remembers that he grew marijuana in his loft. She said she would play among the plants because he told her it was a secret forest where fairies lived, and that's why he had special lights up there. As I get older, I'm starting to realise that there is no such thing as a normal family.

Olivia still hasn't found a job, but I might have convinced her to go back to the office on Monday. Fingers crossed that she does. I think she'll be fine once she's made the first step. If he wants to get rid of her, he'll have to make her redundant, and after all the service she's given to the company, she might get a decent payout.

Jeff sounds very nice. You must tell me all your news about last night. Did he fit in with your friends, okay? Have you seen him on the toilet yet?! Please tell me more news if only to distract me from my situation here. I'm starting to feel like I'm on the set of *Prisoner Cell Block H*—unable to go out in case anyone sees me and I have to lie to their face and unable to take visitors. It honestly feels like solitary confinement or I should be handling a large steaming press and swearing at all the 'screws'.

Speak soon.

Jane

x

To: jane-hubbard@skycorres.co.uk
From: daisyduke71@gomail.com
Date: Sunday, 3rd January 15:16

Dear Jane,

Well, I'm not going to lie; I thought she would have gone by now. I thought she would miss the mock Tudor sweeping drive, and I thought she might miss Derek. For all his faults, she was with him for a while, and he is Ben's dad at the end of the day. Still, I don't know her or Derek, for that matter. What is it about that bloke? I'd love to meet him and tell him what a little turd he is. Only an idiot would let his partner and child down, and he managed to do it twice. As our Cheryl would say, "He must be tucking it into his sock because his face wouldn't make you smile."

Jeff and I had a lovely New Year. Carol, up the road, has a party every year, and half of the town ends up there by midnight. She's a lovely host and always puts on a good night. Jeff felt quite at home there and was talking to a man who recognised him and began to tell him about all of Jeff's work that he had bought over the years. I must admit, I felt like I was out with a celebrity, but he keeps insisting he's an accountant and just dabbles with his art every now and again.

I asked him to stay (on the couch), but he said he couldn't trust himself and would drive home. He's very nice, but I'm keeping my guard up. I have Dad living with me now, so having a man over to stay would be really awkward. I know I'm a middle-aged woman, but no one wants to get frisky when they know their dad is next door or downstairs singing 'I Could Be So Good For You' from *Minder*. So I'm going to take it easy with this one. I'm not going to jump into bed with him like I did with Dean, the Daring Dumper from Didsbury.

You should try the dating app once your life has settled down. I know there are a lot of weirdos out there, but they're not all strange. A lot of them are normal, like you and me—if we are normal, that is. Our Cheryl did my profile. I'm sure she would help you too if you wanted, or are things developing with the local vicar? You might have to wait for a week or two, as she's not speaking to me at the moment because I wouldn't babysit last night. I told her she needed to find some other childcare for the evenings, as she couldn't rely on me anymore. I suggested she offers a teenager some money to sit with them, but she said she thinks it's awful that she has to pay when a perfectly good grandmother is up the road and can do it for nothing. I had to remind her that the point was I couldn't do it, paid or not! She hung up on me, or her credit ran out. I can't tell. But she'll be in touch soon when she realises that the kids are going back to school in a few days and she needs money for shoes for Sharpay, and both of the boys need a new winter coat. Our Bruno's is so tight across the back I thought he left the coat hanger in it when I picked him up from school just before they broke up for Christmas.

I recall us saying that we would catch up in January, but I think we should shelve it for now until we know what's happening with Olivia. I just need a couple of weeks' notice so I can get our Ruth over to sit with Dad. He's getting worse. He woke me up the other night asking me where his car keys were as he needed to go to work. We sold his car years ago, but I couldn't tell him that. I told him to go back to bed, as he'd forgotten he'd put some holidays in and didn't need to go to work that day. Now I have to take the car keys to bed as well as the remote control. I'll be strapping him to the bed before long, like the child out of *The Exorcist*.

I'll go now. Make sure that you get out. Don't stay cooped up, even if it's just to go and see Myla. The newborn stage doesn't last long.

Lots of love

Daisy

xxx

To: daisyduke71@gomail.com
From: jane-hubbard@skycorres.co.uk
Date: Monday, 11th January 20:38

Dear Daisy

What an eventful week it's been. So, Olivia found a little bit of confidence in a large vodka and went to work last Monday, where she was promptly pulled into Derek's office. He said he was surprised that she had the audacity to walk in. She said she was surprised that was the first thing he said and not how his son was. Anyway, she refused to leave and told him that if he wanted to get rid of her, then he would need a good reason to sack her or he would have to make her redundant, and she would welcome the latter. He said that was not an option, and when she challenged him, he simply said it was all a little complicated.

Well, straight away, I presumed that he must have financial issues. I mean, surely keeping two homes and supporting two families would have been a bit of a burden. So we applied to Companies House to get the lowdown on the financial state of his company, and you'll never guess what we found. The company is in her name, and she had no idea. So she called Derek's accountant, Neil, who's always had a soft spot for Olivia. She said that he used to ask her out constantly and only gave up when she became pregnant with Ben, and she was sure he'd tell her what she wanted to know as long as she gave him something in return. I told her that might be a step too far, but she assured me that he would babble enough with a simple meal out. Well, you should have heard her purring on the phone. He jumped at the chance, and she made it clear that she wasn't with Derek anymore. I could literally hear him panting down the line.

Well, she went out with him last night and, cut a long story short, Derek changed the ownership of the company over to Olivia so I couldn't get my hands on it during the divorce. Her signature had been forged, and a dummy transaction had been documented to show a 'sale'. He planned to sell the company back to himself at a later date, and no one would've been any of the wiser.

So she can't make herself redundant, as she's the owner of the business, and she's well within her rights to make him redundant. Neil was quick to point out that there is no employment contract between him and the company, so technically, he doesn't work there, and if he doesn't work there, then she has no obligation to pay him anything. She can, however, get him investigated for fraud and God knows what else. Neil suggested she should 'keep digging'. The funny thing is, I never went after his business during the divorce. I only wanted the house, and now I know why he was so agreeable to my terms.

She's still going to work for now. She wants to do some more investigating before she reveals she knows anything. She's also keeping the accountant in her pocket, so if Derek makes any financial moves, then no doubt Neil will tell her. She's promised him all kinds, including not revealing that he's been a rich source of information. Men, eh? Flash them a bit of cleavage and they can't keep their jaw still. I bet Judas blew Jesus up because some bird promised him a grope in Galilee.

Julian called the other day wanting to come and visit. I said it wasn't convenient as I was sorting the linens. He sounded disappointed, and when I pushed him, he said he was a little worried about his father. He said he keeps visiting them, and they note that Olivia is always busy and can't accompany him. But Julian is worried, as he said Derek looks ill. I told him it was likely to be his irritable bowel; it always flares up after Christmas. I think he believed me. But maybe Olivia leaving him has taken its toll. I haven't told Olivia. Do you think I should?

I've had a think about joining a dating app. I must admit, I'm a little scared, especially after Himesh. I told Olivia about it; she thought it was a splendid idea and said I didn't have to treat it like I was looking for a relationship. She said it would be good for my self-esteem. I've not told her about Dominic. Not that anything is going on. But I will admit that I've had a couple of fantasies about him. They mostly involve aprons, holy red wine and a loud prayer halfway through. I'll say no more than that!

I'm glad you said about visiting. I'm disappointed that I can't accommodate you, but I simply don't have the room. I've given Olivia a room of her own, and Ben still has the small room. The other is the nursery. Once they're gone, you must drive down. I'll need you to get my head straight after all this. I don't need a psychiatrist. I just need you.

Jane

x

To: jane-hubbard@skycorres.co.uk
From: daisyduke71@gomail.com
Date: Sunday, 24th January 20:42

Dear Jane,

I'm sorry it's been a couple of weeks since I've been in touch. To cut to the chase, Dad has had a major stroke. I've been up the hospital most days or nights. Ruth and I try and take it in turns to see him. I was in the kitchen baking as Ruth and I realised we couldn't manage a day out together like we have in the past, and when I asked him if he wanted a cuppa, I found him in a terrible state.

So he's still in hospital and rigged up to anything that has a plug, but it's not looking good. Every time the phone goes, my heart's in my mouth. I must say, our Cheryl has been a good girl. While she finds it difficult to go into hospital because of the kids, she comes to mine and cooks me a little meal for when I come back from visiting Dad. She even changed my bedding the other day, which surprised me. She's not the best at noting how long bedding has been on the bed for. When she lived at home, I would almost have to get the potato peeler to get the sheet off the bed.

My work has been amazing and got me in touch with all kinds of people for support, but until we know exactly what we're dealing with, I'm not sure what to do. Ruth said I can't bring him home, as he'll need a full-time carer. I'm not sure I can afford to give up work, and to be honest, I don't really want to. I'm only fifty-nine, even though I look about eighty.

I've not seen Jeff since Dad took poorly. He texts every day, though, which is nice. But I think he may lose his patience soon. I mean, he's gone on the app to look for part-time fun, not a full-time carer.

I'll keep in touch but forgive me if you don't hear from me for a while.

Love

Daisy

xxx

To: daisyduke71@gomail.com
From: jane-hubbard@skycorres.co.uk
Date: Monday, 25th January, 11:00

Dear Daisy

Always here for you.

Jane

x

To: jane-hubbard@skycorres.co.uk
From: daisyduke71@gomail.com
Date: Friday, 5th February 00:36

Dear Jane,

I can't tell you how touched I was that you came to Dad's funeral. All that way, just for a couple of hours. You must have been shattered when you got home Wednesday night—four hours here and four hours back. But thank you, Jane. When I saw you walk into the church, I knew someone was there to look after me. Our Cheryl was in bits, as you could see, but she had Kelvin, and our Ruth still looked like she was in a state of shock, but at least she had Colin to hold her hand. I was walking in and wishing my James was there and saying to myself, how the hell am I going to make it through the service without anyone? And then you walked in like a bloody guardian angel. I'll always appreciate you telling the priest that the music was supposed to be 'Living Years' by Mike and the Mechanics, not 'Living in a Box'. I thought Ruth was going to die when that started blaring out, so thank you.

I'm glad you didn't stay for the reception thing afterwards. No one really stayed long. I think they were all hungover from the night before. Can you believe they didn't leave my house until four a.m. and the hearse was coming at half nine? I could have throttled them all for staying that long. Where were all these mates the last couple of years? They stopped coming when Dad couldn't remember that he worked with them all in Bentley. I completely understand that it must have been frustrating for them to keep explaining, but they even stopped calling, He could have died months ago, and none of them would have been the wiser. I told our Ruth that I was upset by that, but she said that's just men, and they're all a bit crap when it comes to things like that. It was her who called them to say he'd died.

I don't know if you can remember them. They were all sitting to the left of us. There was one, Titch, who was six foot nine; he seemed to be the leader of them all. Dad used to knock about and drink with Titch a lot when we were younger. I remember my first memory of him when I asked him what the clouds smelled like. He laughed and gave me ten pence for sweets. Every time he called on Dad to go to the White Ram to play darts, he would always give me ten-pence piece. I presumed he gave our Ruth one too. But when Titch said goodbye after the funeral, he pressed a ten-pence into my hand, and our Ruth asked why he did that.

I'm not sure if I told you, but I asked the funeral home to bring Dad home for the last night. That's why the boys were here. They played cards over his coffin, dealt him a hand and between the five of them, they managed to drink three bottles of whisky except for one glass, which sat on his coffin all night.

They told stories all night. Some I'd heard before, but some I hadn't, and Godfrey, who was their foreman, had some very funny tales. And they all admitted they had a crush on Mum. They said he was lucky to have had her and that he was the luckiest of them all. Quite ironic, as he was the only one in a box. Still, at least he's with Mum now.

When they came back a few hours later to see the hearse collect him, they handed me the whisky that had been sitting on the coffin and told me to drink it. I did. I'm glad you weren't here when they carried him out, though. All the Bentley boys insisted that they would put him in the back of the hearse, but Titch, being the height he is, had them all shouting at him to squat down. He had to walk like a cross between a Russian dancer and Groucho bloody Marx to level the coffin out. I'm sure Dad would have laughed.

The house is so empty without him. I know I was on my own before he came, but I got used to him very quickly. I put *Minder* on this morning and left it on while stripping his bed upstairs. I'm not sure what to do with all of his stuff, so I've just shut the door to his room for now. No doubt the day will come when I go back in there and maybe feel a little different. But there's no rush, is there?

I can't sleep at the moment, which is why I'm emailing you so late. I think the worry over the past few months has knocked me all over the place. My manager said she could ask one of the doctors for a prescription for sleeping tablets, but I'm not going down that road. If I get desperate, I'll go to Ruth's and talk to Colin for half an hour. He'd put anyone in a coma with his inane drivel.

Anyway, thanks again for coming up and for all your love and support.

Love

Daisy

xxx

To: daisyduke71@gomail.com
From: jane-hubbard@skycorres.co.uk
Date: Friday, 12th February 18:03

Dear Daisy

I didn't reply any sooner, as I know you would've felt the pressure to email me back. So I thought I would leave you for a week. I just want to email you and tell you that you are in my thoughts and prayers. I've also asked Dominic to say some special prayers for you, which he said he has done and will continue to do.

As I said, you don't need to reply straight away. I will leave you alone.

Jane

x

To: jane-hubbard@skycorres.co.uk
From: daisyduke71@gomail.com
Date: Thursday, 11th March 09:42

Dear Jane,

First, can I say thank you for your prayers and ask you to pass my gratitude to Dominic? He doesn't even know me, which makes it even sweeter of him. How are things going with him these days? Any fantasies come true yet? Or are you holding out for the phone app offerings? Some of them are more than dodgy. Before I met Jeff, I was contacted by a man who, by the second text, asked how I felt about using a sex swing and orgies? I said I'd never experienced either of them and that I could feel nauseous using a revolving door, but regardless of the fact he was that forward by his second text and he looked like Danny DeVito on crack, he should take it down a notch and brush his teeth as he was no Hugh Heffner. So just be careful; there're some weirdos out there.

But there are some lovely ones too. Jeff came over yesterday unannounced. He said he was worried about me and simply wanted to make sure I was okay. He only stayed for a coffee, and when he left, he looked really nervous. He then asked if I was still interested in him, and I told him I was. I just wasn't that much fun to be around. I told him he should find someone else, but he wouldn't hear of it. He said that even though we had only known each other for a short time, he really liked me and was happy to stay in the background until I was ready. It was then I realised he really is a lovely bloke, so I told him to keep Saturday free, and we could do something if I was up to it.

Maybe getting out is what I need to do. I'm going back to work next week, if only for a distraction. I'm just wandering around the house like a bloody ghost, wondering what to do with myself. I know I could go to Cheryl's, but she's been wailing like a banshee since she lost her grandad, and God forgive me, but it gets on my nerves. She didn't have that much time for him when he was alive. She just saw him as someone who brought a halt to her social life. So, until I have the strength to tell her to wind her neck in, I'll just be giving her a wide berth.

Sorry for the miserable email. Tell me all your news.

Lots of love

Daisy

xx

To: daisyduke71@gomail.com
From: jane-hubbard@skycorres.co.uk
Date: Thursday, 11th March 17:04

Dear Daisy

I was starting to worry about you as I'd not heard from you in so long. It sounds like you have had a tough month. I do hope you're getting some support. I know you said you're keeping Cheryl at arm's length, but how about your sister Ruth? I'm sure she's feeling the same as you. She looked after him for a while too. She may have had the same empty feeling when he left hers and went to live with you. But regardless, I'm always here for you.

Well, you wanted some distracting news. There have been a few developments since we last spoke. First being that Derek knows that Olivia was seeing Neil, the accountant. It seems he blabbed and bragged about it when he went in to do an audit. Derek wanted to know how much he'd told Olivia, but he kept quiet about that. The next thing, Derek sacked him and said he didn't feel he was giving him sound advice and would seek someone else's services. Neil was not happy and said he wondered who he could get to do his accounts or half accounts as Derek wouldn't give him all the records he needed. Neil would do some and Derek would finish them off, but Neil always said there was obviously more shadiness going on, but he didn't dig much, as he didn't feel the need to.

Well, Olivia realised he had come to the end of his use and told him she didn't want to see him anymore. She gave him some flannel about needing to find herself as she's never been on her own, but you could tell by his face that he knew why she'd dumped him. I felt a little sorry for him and told her so after he left. She texted him a few days later and asked him if it would be okay if they stayed in touch, and she was sure they would connect again once she had her life settled. It seems he was more than happy with that, and the kisses returned to the end of his texts. I doubt she will contact him, but in the meantime, he lives in hope, and he may find someone else to number crunch with.

Olivia is still going to work, and she said it's not too bad now. Derek doesn't interact with her at all; he only talks about Ben. They're still negotiating child support (she's not seen a penny yet). Do you know, he's not even asked where they're living?

She's been trying to find more account records but keeps hitting a brick wall. It seems the staff in his accounts department are all very loyal to him and have instantly shown their allegiance to their leader. Apparently, a lot of the staff in his company are blanking her. I'm not sure I could work in that environment every day, but she says she was never that popular anyway. It's a shame I don't know anyone in there now who could help.

She still hasn't told him that she knows the company is in her name. She said she's waiting for the right time. I asked her when that would be, but she said she didn't know. She just couldn't stop thinking about how Neil told her to keep digging. But how many holes do you have to dig to realise that there's no treasure to be found?

Ben is still going to his old school, which is a bit of a run, but even I agreed with her that it was best for him. He's had enough upheaval without changing schools too. I read him a bedtime story the other day, and he asked me if his mum and dad would ever live in the same house again. I told him to ask his mum but asked if he was missing his dad. He said he did, but not now. He said he only misses Lena, the nanny. How sad is that? He asked if he could stay in our house forever, as he loved how I cooked chicken pie because I let him crimp the pastry and stab the middle. He loves being in the kitchen with me. Olivia takes him to school before work, then I pick him up and he does his homework while I finish a bit of work admin. We then both start the evening meal while we wait for his mum to come home.

She said the other day that she has enough put by for a deposit to rent a flat. When I asked her about furniture, she said she would have to ask Derek for some things from the house in Lyndhurst. I'm not holding out much hope for that. Does she not realise when he pulls a ten-pound note out, the queen has to put her sunglasses on? She keeps saying that she can't impose on me much longer, and the fact that I'm still keeping her a secret is not fair, as I can't have Julian over.

I will admit, Daisy, I don't want her to go. I've actually become quite fond of her. When we put Ben to bed, we sometimes open a bottle of Prosecco and compare stories not just about Derek but about life. I think the chats are helping her self-esteem, to be honest. But she's doing me some good as well. There was me thinking that they had this marvellous life, but she said most of the time, he was in work or at meetings, and when he was home, he just wanted to play with his model railway set that he'd set up in the attic. He always said it was for Ben, but Ben wasn't allowed to touch it, so the child stopped asking in the end and played with her or Lena. She also said that he's only ever taken her on one holiday, which was to the Cayman Islands last year, and the whole time he was there, he was working and had to go to meetings. As far as she was aware, they had no contacts in the Caribbean, so she suspected he was just going for long walks to get away from her and Ben. He really is an arsehole.

I've not told her that I'd like her to stay. Part of me thinks she has to find her own way. But another part of me wouldn't mind just telling Julian she's here and getting it over and done with. I'm not sure what to do for the best, and all the while this has been happening, Derek has been texting me incessantly. I'm only keeping him away from the house as he thinks I have a fancy man here all the time. He keeps saying he wants us to be friends and still has lots of feelings for me. I asked him if Olivia knew he was texting me all the while, but he never answered. He just keeps talking about the old days when he was with me like they were the best days of his life, which they probably were seeing as he was getting his leg over Olivia as well as me. I did wonder where he found all the energy but then realised in our last year of marriage, I only had two orgasms, and one of them was prompted by seeing Tom Ellis's backside on *Lucifer*. From some of the late-night chats I've had with Olivia, I don't think she fared much better, especially when she asked me what vibrator did I prefer? Prefer? I've never owned one! Do you?

Julian and Carrie have found their groove with Myla. She's such a good baby, and it's so lovely to see Julian finally relax with her. I go to their house when I want to see them. I keep telling them it's easier for me to come to them while Myla is so small and needs so much stuff. At the moment, Julian agrees, but I worry about how long this will last. In the meantime, I try and pop over a couple of times a week and help them with washing and cooking a meal while they take her out. Sometimes they leave her with me while they get some shopping. I've told them they should stay out and have some lunch in a pub somewhere, but they never take me up on it. They say Myla would fret for them, but as we both know, the baby probably doesn't have a clue at this age. After saying that, Julian seems to have the knack for settling her quickly. He lays her over his thigh and gently rocks her from side to side, and if he hums the theme tune to *Question Time*, she's out like a light.

Anyway, that's enough for now. I'll fill you in more in a few days. Sending you lots of love, my friend.

Love

Jane

x

To: jane-hubbard@skycorres.co.uk
From: daisyduke71@gomail.com
Date: Monday, 15th March 20:11

Dear Jane,

Well, I went back to work today. I was dreading it, but to be honest, it was good to be back and focus my mind on other things. Everyone was trying to be sweet, asking how I was, but it wasn't until they started apologising that I realised that none of them had come to Dad's funeral. It's not like they knew him, but they've known me for years, and you would have thought one of them would have turned up. Maybe it's one of those things that happens when you work from home. I did get a card, so I guess I have to be grateful for that.

I was going to go round to our Cheryl's tonight, but once I'd done my shift, I couldn't be bothered. Kelvin texted me around three this afternoon to make sure I was still coming. I think he wants me to get a grip of Cheryl. He said she's in a deep state of depression and hasn't done a thing in the house because of it. As the afternoon wore on, I just knew that I was going to walk into chaos, and Kelvin would be expecting me to straighten the house or Cheryl's head or both. I don't have the energy for either. I felt like I needed a lie down after opening a tin of minestrone soup for my lunch.

What's up with me, Jane? I can't be bothered doing anything. Even though I was in work today, I didn't really do a tap— not that there was much to do anyway. I didn't even see Jeff on Saturday. He offered to take me for a drive to get me out of the house, but I said if I wanted to get out, I have a perfectly good garden. I realised as I walked around the garden that might be the last time I hear from him. I also realised my garden is that overgrown, I wouldn't have been surprised if an Amazonian native shot a dart at me.

Well anyway, your news. Have you told Olivia yet to leave or not to leave? Could you not encourage her to find somewhere close so you could still be involved with Ben? I'm sure she'd be glad of the help, as it seems you're her only support at the moment. What you and her ever did see in Derek is beyond me. But look, at the end of the day, what you decide to do will be the right decision and blow Derek and Julian. We women always paint the other woman as a bitch, but I've come to realise that life is very complicated, and so are feelings. Sometimes we understand why we feel the way we do, as in my case, but then sometimes things happen that go against all convention, and instead of doing what we feel is right and what would make us happy, we end up doing things simply because it's what everyone else expects. But is it? So you do whatever makes you happy and blow everyone else. Life is short.

Has Olivia decided how she's going to play things with Derek? Have you guys not formulated a plan yet? If I was her, I think I would have gone in and strung his bollocks up like a pair of onions by now.

I'll go now. Sorry again for another miserable email. I'm sure by my next email, I will feel a lot brighter.

Love

Daisy

xxx

To: daisyduke71@gomail.com
From: jane-hubbard@skycorres.co.uk
Date: Wednesday, 17th March 19:19

Dear Daisy

Thanks for your sage words in the last email. You're always full of advice. So because of that, I ended up chatting with Olivia last night. I told her how I felt about her and Ben staying with me and gave her the option of staying, and if she didn't want that, I suggested she gets something close by. She said she was also thinking and had talked to Ben about it too. After all, what she decides affects him, and she said she didn't want him looking back and thinking that he was pulled from pillar to post and no one had considered his feelings. Well, apparently, he wants to stay in the house. He said he loves it, and I still haven't shown him how to bake meringue yet. He may only be a little boy, but he's not stupid. Olivia said it wasn't a good idea and they needed to find somewhere else to live, but now I've told her what I think she said she needs a few days to mull it over.

She's off out on Friday night after work for a leaving do. She was in two minds about going as most people don't like her, but the girl who's leaving said she should go. She asked me what she should do if Derek decides to go. I told her to wear a backless dress and flirt with every man in Derek's eyeline. She laughed.

In other news, Dominic asked me to go to Bath with him at the weekend. He wants to visit a deacon who's been told he's terminally ill. He suggested he drops me in the centre for an hour while he sees him. I think I may go. The last time I was there, I was mistaken for Celina Imrie, so I have pleasant memories of the place. He said I need to tell him by tomorrow so he can sort cover for the Sunday services.

I'll let you know how it all goes over the weekend.

Jane

x

To: jane-hubbard@skycorres.co.uk
From: daisyduke71@gomail.com
Date: Monday, 22nd March 20:44

Dear Jane,

How did your weekend go in Bath? I hope you had a wonderful time. I was out myself this weekend. Jeff turned up on my doorstep Saturday morning and insisted I get ready as he was taking me out. I tried to say no, but he pretended to be annoyed with me and refused to go. Well, in the end, we went to Blackpool. We walked along the beach, and he told me that when he was younger, he would stay there with his uncle every summer. Apparently, his mum and dad were always fighting, so he would go to his uncle's to get away from it all. He said it was his uncle who supported him while he did his maths degree and was the only one who went to his graduation. His uncle has gone now, but he said the place was very special to him, and that's why he wanted to take me. I felt very flattered, and I'm not sure it was entirely true, but you know what men are like. They'll say anything if they think that they're going to get lucky. A man once told me that I was his first girlfriend, but then I found out he had a string of exes, and one was still wearing his engagement ring. I still married him, though, and we had thirty-odd very happy years together.

Jeff agreed with me about keeping our Cheryl at arm's length for a while when he noticed me ignoring her calls. He said she had Kelvin there who could look after her, but who did I have? When I said no one, he asked if he could do it for a little while. I realised that since I married James, all I've done is look after people—James, our Cheryl, the grandkids, and then Dad. Let's face it, our Cheryl might have left home, but she's never really gone away, has she? I wanted to melt into his arms. It would have been so easy, but I have to find the strength on my own. What if he finds someone nicer on the app, and then I'm left with grief and a broken heart to boot? I just have to be careful.

He came over on Sunday, too, and took me to Manchester for lunch. He knew the restaurant owner, who was very nice and explained that Jeff was his summer playmate as he had grown up in Blackpool. He dropped me off early evening, and we've been texting each other a fair bit. Nothing heavy, but it's been nice to say good morning and good night to someone, even if it's just over the phone.

Let me know how it went with Dominic. It sounds like he's growing on you.

Love Daisy

xxx

To: daisyduke71@gomail.com
From: jane-hubbard@skycorres.co.uk
Date: Wednesday, 24th March 19:19

Dear Daisy

Well, I have a fair bit to tell you. First, I'll tell you about Olivia. As I said, she was invited to a leaving do. The girl who was leaving told Olivia that she was leaving as she suspected dodgy dealings were going on with the accounts. She'd been there for years and started to suspect things a while back but put it down to lack of experience and didn't do anything. Anyway, someone called Demi, who works there too, got very drunk and was bragging about having discovered Derek was fiddling the accounts so he didn't have to pay tax and was hiding assets.

Olivia made a beeline for Demi and pretended to be really pally with her, buying vodka for them both, though Olivia's was water. She acted drunk and started to tell Demi all about how shit Derek was in bed, that she was only staying with him for the money and planned to chuck him out soon. The next thing, Demi was telling her everything about how she'd confronted him and told him she'd keep her mouth shut providing he gave her a hush payment each month. She claimed she was keeping a second set of books for him.

On Saturday, Olivia got hold of Neil, the accountant (I think I should just call him Neil), who told her that she still needed to find proof of it all. Needless to say, when they went back to work on Monday, Demi was giving Olivia a wide berth, which Olivia let run for a couple of days, and then today, she asked Demi out to lunch. Demi said she was busy, but Olivia insisted.

Over the lunch, Olivia revealed that she'd been sober on the night out and remembered everything Demi had told her. Olivia revealed that she knew things already, but there were some missing pieces, which she felt Demi could help her with, and she told her she wanted to see the 'other' books. When Demi refused, Olivia said that someone was already investigating the company and they hadn't found a connection to Demi or blackmail, but it was only a matter of time. This sent the girl into a panic, of course, so Olivia said she would help keep her out of trouble if she sent her the accounts. She had them within the hour, and they go back years!

It looks like they started around the same time he started seeing Olivia. Clearly, having two women in your life is an expensive affair. Maybe he thought divorcing me would stop all that nonsense. So now Olivia has all these accounts and is not sure what to do with them. She contacted Neil, who said he didn't want to be involved as he may be implicated, and the fact that he was let go would suggest a revenge attack. He just wished her all the best.

The trouble is we don't know who to trust with all this, and to be honest, Olivia doesn't know what she wants out of it. I think getting the house is enough, but she feels she should have a share in the company, as she helped it grow by expanding its services and bringing in a whole host of major clients. These clients still will only deal with her, and a lot of them don't like Derek, so if she goes, so will the clients, and then the company will go too. She just wants to think about it for now and see what her options are, but I think she's wasting time. What's to stop Demi from leaving and giving Derek the heads-up before she goes?

In other news, Julian and Carrie have booked the christening for the end of May. I'm sure it will be a quiet affair. They don't have many friends, as you know. It would be lovely if you could come, and Jeff, of course, if he's still on the scene. He sounds like a really nice man, and it's nice to know that someone is looking after you. I know you miss your dad terribly.

I went to Bath with Dominic. We had a lovely day. He drove in his car, which is a Nissan Note. It would have been far more comfortable in my Mercedes Benz, but I didn't want him to feel overwhelmed by my leather interior and walnut dashboard, so I kept my mouth shut. He didn't drop me in the town; I went to the old deacon's house with him instead. I was surprised to discover that he already knew who I was. It seems Dominic has been telling him all about me. When I questioned Dominic about it later in the day, he insisted that he tells the deacon of everyone in the congregation. I'm not sure. Or is that me just being big-headed?

The deacon was lovely, and we talked for a couple of hours. I found out during the course of the conversation that Dominic comes from a very large family. Most of them live in Devon except for a brother who lives near Newcastle and another who emigrated to Australia three years ago. The deacon teased Dominic about him not being married, which Dominic found uncomfortable. He said he hadn't met the right woman, but the deacon said he wouldn't be so sure of that and looked directly at me. Dominic apologised for that later during the drive home. I was close to telling him that I didn't mind the suggestion, but then it would make it awkward, and I still wasn't sure how he felt when I told a joke about faking orgasms and the *Antiques Roadshow*. I'm not sure if I could be with anyone who can't see the humour in a dirty joke. Honestly, I'm not even sure I could be with a vicar. But after saying that, we did have a few laughs during the day, and I've asked him over Friday night to make him a meal. I might dig out my Nigella cookbook. I haven't cooked from that, as I always felt telling anyone that I cooked from it would suggest that it could be construed as foreplay.

I'm dying to hear about how things are developing with Jeff. The christening is set for the last bank holiday in May. I'll leave it up to you if you want to bring Jeff—or anyone else, for that matter. I've asked Olivia if she could share with Ben while you're here, and she said that would be fine, but she suspects she'll be gone by then.

Jane

x

To: jane-hubbard@skycorres.co.uk
From: daisyduke71@gomail.com
Date: Sunday, 28th March 11:01

Dear Jane,

How are you? Sorry I've not been in touch all week, but I wanted to check something before I got back to you. Now, I know you may not be happy with me, but I thought it was worth taking the risk. I need to tell you that I told Jeff all about you, Olivia, Derek and the dodgy accounts, and he said he'd be more than happy to look them over. He was quite passionate about wanting to help. He said his dad ripped off his mum during the divorce, and when he died, he left all his money to a woman he'd only been with for ten months. He said it wasn't about the money; it was the fact he wasn't even acknowledged. He suggested I give you his email and you or Olivia reach out to him.

I know you may be cross with me for breaking your confidence, but I trust Jeff. He has a lot of love in his life, which tells me he's a good bloke and people like being around him. You only like being around people you can trust. He won't be insulted if you don't take him up on the offer. He's not like that, so don't worry if I bring him to Myla's christening. He said he's seen lots of cases like this and people think that they're clever at hiding stuff, but like he said, there's no grey area with maths. If it doesn't add up, it's either incompetence, carelessness or dodgy dealings. The first two you can eliminate quite quickly, which really will only leave you with the latter. His email address is J.Powell@gomail.com. I'll leave it up to you.

Still talking of Jeff, we went out last night. Nothing fancy. We just went to the local pub and grabbed something to eat. Jeff being Jeff, of course, knew someone in there. But he's such a gent, and while saying he was glad to see them, he still made it clear that he was out with me. I told him that he could stay in Dad's bed so he could have a drink. Well, he ended up coming back to mine, and I asked him to get in the bed with me. It wasn't for sex; I wanted some human contact. I just wanted a cuddle. But this morning, he got up early, made me some breakfast and climbed back in bed to chat with me while I ate. When he seemed satisfied that I'd eaten all my breakfast, he went to get up, and I asked him to stay. He did for most of the day.

He was so gentle and loving, and afterwards, he just held me. I have to say that it felt comfortable. I haven't felt that comfortable since James died. It wasn't just comfort; I felt safe. Does that make sense? I'm so bloody confused, Jane. I know there have been a few men since James, but they were all a bit of fun. This is different. This man really cares about me, and when I'm with him, I feel scared of my feelings, but when I'm not, I start to miss him and want him to come back. It's so strange. And as much as I loved James, I'm not sure if he ever made me feel like this. James and I had an expected love, I suppose. We were courting that long it was just expected that we would get married and have a family. I'm not sure I can say how I feel about Jeff, but I know it's different.

Anyway, I finally went to see Cheryl this week. The grandkids were so excited to see me and asked if they could come back, seeing as Pops was gone. I told them that they could maybe come next week. I heard Cheryl tell the kids when they were in the kitchen to unpack their bags. Cheryl has been far from moping around the house. It seems she's been out a few times with Jade and went to an Ann Summers party the other day. Kelvin insisted it was to help with her depression. I'm sure he's right. I mean, who do you know doesn't smile after a satisfactory session with a vibrator? Talking of which, I cannot believe you've never had one. I've made a mental note to buy you one for your birthday or Christmas. Trust me, the first time you decide to use it, make sure you have nothing planned for a couple of days afterwards. You'll spend a day blowing your mind and need the other to get your breath back. Our Cheryl's mate bought one from a website, and she said it was so powerful it came with a warning and an application form to apply for a blue disabled badge. But I think it's safe to say our Cheryl has gotten over the worst of her grandad's passing. I stayed firm when she whined for me to take the kids; even Kelvin took me to one side and begged me to take them.

Sorry, I forgot to say earlier that Jeff and I will be coming to the christening. Don't worry if Olivia is still there; we can get a hotel. Let's just see where we all are the week before and take it from there.

When I come down, it would be nice to see Dominic. Will Myla be christened in his church? I'd like to meet him properly without the robes and smell of incense. I'm not anti-church, but whenever I go into one, it feels like when a cop car is behind you. You know you've done nothing wrong but instantly feel guilty about something. That's how I feel when I go into a church, like God's looking down at me, saying, *"I know you robbed that Merrydown cider from the Kwik Save when you were younger."* Then a big lightning bolt will fry the top of my head, and everyone will see my smoke of guilt. Irrational, I know, but that's just me.

I'll go now. I promised our Cheryl I would go over and help her cook a Sunday roast, which means she'll watch while I do it. I'm not sure if it's because of Dad passing or because of her behaviour when he was alive, but I've got a bit wiser to some of her antics. Cheryl always knew how to wrap me around her finger, but no more. When I told her about Jeff, she said that's why I've changed, and she's not sure if Jeff is having a good effect on me. As soon as she said that, I knew he must be a good man. I do love our Cheryl, but the only things she's attracted to are lousy men and midwives.

I'll tell Jeff I've given you his email details. No pressure.

Love

Daisy

xxx

To: daisyduke71@gomail.com
From: jane-hubbard@skycorres.co.uk
Date: Tuesday, 6th April 18:45

Dear Daisy

Has Jeff spoken to you about his conversation with Olivia today? She is so grateful that he's going to help her. She said he sounded charming on the phone and really thinks that he will be able to help her. I think she may be in her room now, sending everything over. Demi was dragging her feet with it all, but when Olivia told her that they were investigating him as far as Liverpool, Demi drained to the colour of a rice pudding.

Derek called her into his office the other day and said he was still surprised she was working there. He even hinted at redundancy, which Olivia laughed at. He actually asked after Ben and where she was living. She told him that if he wanted to see Ben, he was to call him first and see how Ben felt about it. She's not mentioned it to the child, which is just as well, as the phone call hasn't transpired yet. I don't know how Derek can ignore him. He's so precious and funny; it made me realise that Julian was far too serious as a child. Maybe he got that from Derek.

Fun to Julian when he was younger was letter writing. He would write to the BBC, complain about the quality of their programming schedule, and come up with suggestions. He even told BBC Director Greg Dyke that he was missing a trick in not hiring Anne Diamond and Jennie Bond for any presenting and that they could be the new Ant and

Dec. He was also constantly writing to the prime minister asking for comparison reports of leaving or remaining within the EU. He was only twelve. Looking back, I blame myself more than Derek. I should have encouraged him to play out more and make friends with the children that lived nearby. But Derek didn't like seeing children playing out. He said if he wanted to see children playing, he would have bought a house on *Sesame Street*. The fact that it's a fictional place and in America didn't sway him when anyone argued with him.

On another note, Julian finally let me have Myla overnight at the weekend. They'd been invited to a wedding in Kent, and the bride was quite implicit about not having children there, especially four-month-old babies. It took some convincing, but they eventually said it was okay when I was challenged on my credentials. I simply said that the fact Julian was still alive was surely a testament that I could look after a child.

I said I would look after her in their house, which seemed easier than dragging all of her equipment over to my house. I'm not sure I could fit the cot, play centre, bath, clothes, bottles, bottle-cleaning equipment, toiletries, nappies, lunch chair and enough clothes to shoot an episode of *The Clothes Show* into the boot of my Mercedes. Unbeknown to Julian, Olivia and Ben came over for the night, after all, Ben is Myla's uncle, not that he knows. Olivia and I thought it was terribly sweet to watch him feeding her. They even had a bath together, and she giggled at him when he threw water over his face. They left early in the morning, as I suspected Julian and Carrie would leave at the first crack of light. I do worry, though, how much Olivia and I keep telling Ben that everything is a secret. He knows not to ever tell his father about me or the fact that they're living in my house.

They missed each other by forty minutes, which gave me enough time to straighten up the spare room. I'm not sure they would have noticed anyway. Carrie swooped on the baby as soon as she walked in. You wouldn't think that they'd been gone for a fortnight. The scene was worthy of an episode of *Long Lost Family*.

Keep me in the loop if Jeff finds anything out. I've got a horrible feeling about all of this.

Jane

x

To: jane-hubbard@skycorres.co.uk
From: daisyduke71@gomail.com
Date: Thursday, 8th April 22:41

Dear Jane,

Jeff's just left. He came over this morning and worked from here all day. He hardly raised his head all day. I don't know anything just yet, but there were a lot of 'Jesus Christs' being mumbled under his breath. When I asked him what was going on, he said he needed a bit more time to get his head around it all. I asked him if it was too much seeing as he was doing it for free, but he was quite insistent that all was fine and he wanted to help. He said he would come back tomorrow as long as it was okay for him to work from my house. I quite like the company, to be honest.

Our Cheryl met him yesterday. She turned up unannounced to ask if I would have the kids over the weekend but was surprised to see Jeff sitting at the dining room table with his laptop. When I told her that I was still not up for having the kids overnight just yet, she got stroppy and said the only reason I was saying no was because I had Jeff staying overnight. She wasn't talking quietly; he could hear the whole thing through the serving hatch. I told her what I did in my own house was my own business, and I would happily have the kids for the day or even babysit for them in her house, but the days of me picking them up from school on a Friday and them not going home until Sunday are long gone. She looked shocked and flounced off. I still can't be dealing with her moods. It's like she's grown up but has forgotten she's an adult now with her own family.

I'll make up with her one day, but for now, I'm keeping her arm's length again. Jeff is still being very sweet to me. Having him in the house and working opposite me has been so nice. I asked him does he not find me a distraction as he's so used to working on his own. He admitted I was a nice distraction, and that's why he'd like to come back each day while he's investigating Derek's finances. For the first time since Dad's been gone, I've started shopping for two again. He doesn't stay for tea every night, but he's always here at lunchtime and I like to get him corned beef, prawn cocktail crisps and fig rolls. He might be good-looking, but he has no taste. Prawn cocktail crisps?

Sometimes he stays over, which is always lovely. He is so gentle and considerate. Very different from James and Dean. I knew all of James's moves, and Dean wore me out. I think Jeff may have had a few lovers in his past who have all taught him the art of love-making. I never thought at my age, I would still be learning new stuff about myself, but there you go.

I will keep you up to date if Jeff reveals anything about Derek.

Love

Daisy

xx

To: daisyduke71@gomail.com
From: jane-hubbard@skycorres.co.uk
Date: Sunday, 11th April 20:20

Dear Daisy

Well, what a weekend I've just had. It seems that everyone simply got tired of being kept away from the house.

This morning Olivia, Ben and I were up as usual and having breakfast at nine. I was making pancakes for Ben when the next thing I heard Julian and Carrie walking through the front door. Quick as a flash, Olivia grabbed Ben to hide in the downstairs wet room. We had that installed when I asked Derek if we could sell up and move to a bungalow, as one day we might have trouble tackling the stairs. He said installing a downstairs bathroom was cheaper than paying stamp duty on the next house. I accepted this at the time, but looking back, this would've been when he was buying the house in Lyndhurst with Olivia. Moving a family is stressful enough, but moving two is impossible. I project-managed the wet room conversion (it was originally part of the utility room), and that was that. I never use the room, to be honest. I find it off-putting to see a huge plughole in the middle of the floor.

Anyway, Olivia and Ben made it into the room before Julian walked in and immediately spied the table was set for three. When he asked who was there, I should have said any name and told him they had just left, but instead, I blurted out the truth and shouted to Olivia to come out.

Carrie and Julian were shocked, obviously, and of course, Julian wanted to leave, but I insisted he stayed. When Julian got angry, saying he had to get out, Carrie shouted at him. I've never seen her lose her temper with him before. She said he was acting like a spoiled child, and was this the first impression he wanted to give his little brother? She told him to sit down and listen to me explain what had been going on. They led the conversation, saying they thought I'd moved a fancy man in as I hadn't let them come to the house recently.

Olivia and I told them nearly everything. We didn't mention anything about Derek's finances. The less people know about that, the better for now. We simply said that Olivia had left for personal reasons. Julian became ugly at this point, suggesting that she was having an affair and that his father had thrown her out. I told him that Olivia was an innocent party in it all, and he was to take what detail we gave him at face value and not fill in any missing blanks with details that put Olivia in a bad light. Carrie backed me up, saying that something very unfair must have happened for me to give them a roof over their heads.

Julian settled a bit then but continued like he was doing me a favour when he said he would have a cup of tea. It was at this point Ben asked Olivia what time it was, and when we told him, he said that Myla was due her feed and asked if he could do it. Even Carrie looked shocked, asking how Ben knew Myla's feeding routine. In the end, I had to come clean and say that while they were at the Kent wedding, Olivia and Ben came over and helped me look after the baby. I made a point of saying that Ben was wonderful playing with his niece at bath time and had helped with the feeds. I apologised and said I would have liked to have told the truth at the time, but we weren't sure if Julian would go back and tell his father everything.

At this point, Julian revealed that he hardly spoke to his father since it all came out about Ben and Olivia. Carrie was the one who said that he should not take it out on Ben. We all sat in silence for a bit, munching on pink wafers (Ben's favourite), and then Carrie asked Ben if he would help her with Myla's feed. He did us proud, and Carrie watched in awe at his efficiency in sorting her bib and propping up his cushions to support his arm. Once the feed was finished, Julian asked Ben if he would like to go to the garage with him, as he had some things he would like to show him. Off they went, and we all guessed that Julian was showing him his ventriloquist dummies.

They were still in there when there was a knock at the door, and would you believe who it was? It was Derek! I had to shout about him being there, as he stepped in, and by the time we walked to the kitchen, Olivia had disappeared and Carrie was sitting looking casual with a sleeping Myla. I challenged Derek as to why he had turned up unannounced, and he simply said he was passing. Passing indeed? He probably wanted to see if I had a man in the house. I said he would have to go when there was another knock at the door, and it was Dominic. He decided to pop around in between church services. I whispered to him that Derek was there and could he 'play up' the boyfriend role in front of him?

Dominic walked in like he was very familiar with the place and even embraced Carrie like they were old friends. When Dominic put the kettle on to make himself a drink, he asked if I'd replaced his mug that I'd accidentally smashed the last time he was here. I played along, saying that I was sorry and would get one the next time I passed the shop we both loved in that charming village we stayed one night. It was at this point that Derek said he would go to the garage and see what Julian was doing. Dominic saw the horror on my face and rushed to block Derek's path and insisted that he would ask Julian if he wanted a cup of tea and, while he was there, let him know Derek was here and wouldn't be staying long so he needed to come and see him.

While Dominic was fetching Julian from the garage, Derek was getting wound up, saying who was he to say how long he was staying there for? I told him that Dominic had no right to say that as it was my house and that he was welcome to stay for five minutes and then had to be on his way, as all the disturbance would likely wake Myla. Julian then walked in with Dominic behind. He played it very cool with his father and helped Dominic make the tea while casually asking his father if he often called in unannounced. The amateur dramatic lessons were now paying off. Derek struggled to answer, saying he was simply passing and would be on his way.

When Derek was leaving, he spied Ben's bike by the front door and asked me who the bike belonged to. Quick as a flash, Dominic asked me if it was the bike the neighbour had dropped off for the charity sale at the church, which I said it was and he could take it with him afterwards.

Derek then left, and as I walked him to his car, he said he knew I would have a man around and was shocked that Julian seemed comfortable with him. I told him it's so much easier to introduce people to your family when you haven't been hiding them for eight years, which seemed ironic since they were hiding in my garage at the time.

When I walked back in, Olivia, Ben, Carrie, Julian and Dominic were all relaying their parts in the bizarre scene that had just taken place. As we sat around the kitchen table, they all began to challenge each other on who knew what and how long they had known for. There was a lot of 'I've only just found out'.

How do I get into these situations? Dominic didn't stay for his tea. He excused himself and said I needed to be with my family after a scene like that. I thanked him and said I would see him during the week and would tell him everything that had been happening.

Ben wasn't aware that his dad had been in the house. He was too interested in the dummies, which delighted Julian, of course. They left after an hour, and as they were leaving, Julian and Carrie invited us all over for Sunday lunch next week. Olivia accepted, and Ben asked if he would be able to help with Myla, which Julian said he could.

So there you have it; it's all out now. Well, most of it, and it's such a relief. It's good that Julian and Ben can form a relationship, and it's good that Olivia feels she has some family, but the main thing for me is that Ben has family, and we don't have to keep telling him to keep things secret.

If Derek were on the phone all the while, then it would be a different story, but as he rarely calls the lad, it will be so much easier now.

Well, that's all I can write for now. I'm so tired after such an eventful day.

Jane

x

To: jane-hubbard@skycorres.co.uk
From: daisyduke71@gomail.com
Date: Tuesday, 13th April 19:58

Dear Jane

Your email had me spinning, and I told Jeff about it over a bottle of wine. I must admit we started to laugh about the whole scene and had visions of Derek walking into the garage to find Julian with his hand up Thin Lizzy, who was blabbing the whole story while Julian looked on helplessly as if he had no control, while Carrie came in and started telling Thin Lizzy off as it was none of her business. We got a good half hour out of that, and it was the biggest laugh I've had since we watched that fat Texan on the cruise trying to get into a wetsuit. I'm sorry it was at the expense of your family.

I've just said goodbye to Jeff. He's gone home to Liverpool for a few days to do some other work. I hear he spoke to Olivia yesterday, and she now has the lay of the land and he's given her some options. He said he might need to go to Hampshire and see her. I'm sure she's told you. I don't know anything, and I've not asked, as I appreciate it's confidential. We always said that if I wanted to know anything, then I was to ask you and I understand that.

Only tell me if you can and want to, but I'm itching to know what's happening. Does she have a plan? Is she going to hang him out to dry? Will she ever tell him that you helped her in her hour of need and she's been living under your roof for nearly four months? That's the bit I can't get over.

Where the hell does he think she is? Or does he not think about it at all? How is he not asking her all these questions?

Love Daisy

xxx

To: daisyduke71@gomail.com
From: jane-hubbard@skycorres.co.uk
Date: Sunday, 18ᵗʰ April 21:02

Dear Daisy

Sorry I've not been in touch all week. Olivia and I have been busy making plans, but after saying that, I'm still a little in the dark about it all. All I know is that she's very happy with what Jeff discovered and has agreed to him coming down next Thursday; he will accompany her to the office on Friday, which I'm sure you know. All Olivia keeps saying is that Derek doesn't have a leg to stand on.

She did say that Jeff will want to talk to me when he arrives. She wouldn't say what it was, as Jeff asked her not to. He feels it's best if he explains it himself. I'm not going to lie, Daisy, I have a horrible feeling that I'm going to be implicated in something. I don't know what, and I know I've done nothing wrong, but after the way Derek treated me and Olivia, and especially Ben, I wouldn't put anything past him.

We all went to Julian's today for lunch. Olivia was really nervous about going in case Julian had changed his mind but felt he was forced to continue with the lunch, and for a moment, it wouldn't have surprised me if she was right. Julian, as you know, is a flaky bugger. But when we got there, he was beaming to see us, especially Ben, who brought his football. While Olivia nursed Myla and I helped Carrie with the dinner, Julian and Ben played football in the garden. I've never seen Julian kick a ball in my life, and I had to take myself to the bathroom and cry. Silly, I know. I'm not sure why I was crying, but all I know is that when I watched them from the kitchen window, I saw Julian the same age as Ben. He was laughing and running around with him. Is it any wonder Julian turned out the way he did with Derek and me for parents? But it gives me hope that Myla will have a far more balanced upbringing than her father did, and she'll be far more rounded with the influencers in her life, including Olivia and Ben. I know they've only been in our lives for a few months, but they're family, and I've learned to love them both.

Dinner was lovely, and we laughed so much. I told them your story that you and Jeff made up a scene with Derek and Thin Lizzy having a conversation. They were howling, and Julian had tears streaming down his cheeks. I don't think I've ever seen him like that. He made me promise that when you come to visit I will take you over to their house. He's never said that about any of my friends.

On the way home, Olivia and I talked about what a lovely day it had been and how it seemed silly to have been nervous. I told her that the silliest thing was that if Derek had been upfront about her years ago, we might have had years of days like that. Then we laughed at the absurdity of it and concluded that I would've scratched her eyes out, and she would have scratched up my Mercedes.

Olivia and I put Ben to bed and shared a bottle of Prosecco. She's gone to bed now too, but I'm still a little wired after the day. Over our fizz, we debated how to explain to Ben who Julian actually was. We decided that if we just acted normal and answered his questions, he would eventually realise himself, and by that time, it would all feel normal. So we're not hiding things from him, but we're not coming out and telling him either—a bit like the Liberal Democrats.

I'm looking forward to seeing Jeff, but I'm disappointed that it won't be you introducing him. There'll be the christening, I suppose, when I will see a different Jeff to the one that is coming on Thursday. I know you said he's not given you any information, but has he given you an indication or even a feeling of how I'm tied up in all of this? I think that could be why I'm wired all the time. Is this how people feel on drugs like cocaine? I feel super alert. I heard a baby crying on *Call the Midwife* tonight and shot up out of the chair, thinking it was Myla. I don't think I was this twitchy when Derek was leaving me.

I'm seeing Dominic tomorrow for lunch and then an afternoon walk at Christchurch Bay. I want to buy him lunch to thank him for his fine performance when he was in my house the other day. I'm secretly hoping to pass a shop that sells mugs so I can buy one and tell him that it will live in my cupboard for him. I know it sounds cheesy, but in my head, it looks romantic.

Okay, well, I'd best be off now. Let me know if you hear anything.

Love Jane

x

To: jane-hubbard@skycorres.co.uk
From: daisyduke71@gomail.com
Date: Wednesday, 21st April 11:12

Dear Jane

I hope your nerves haven't got the better of you. It's only a couple more days, and then all of this will be out. I don't know much, but what I do know is that Jeff has all of your interests, and to trust him. That's all I can say. There's no point in me telling you to keep calm because if I were you, I'd be more than wired. Just make sure you stay united with Olivia. From the little Jeff has been allowed to tell me the last couple of days, she is a good girl.

Bet you wish you had that Zen room now and became a Buddhist.

If nothing else, trust me.

Love

Daisy

xxx

Thursday, 22nd April

While Olivia was upstairs touching up her make-up, Jane watched out of the front room window, waiting for a car she didn't recognise to pull up outside her modest detached house. She wondered if she should have tidied the front garden a little but then realised that things like that were no longer important.

Daisy had said very little to her about what was to develop over the next few days. She just knew that she was part of it. If she was arrested for anything, would the police believe her? Would Julian and Carrie, more importantly? Surely, they knew that she didn't have a dishonest bone in her body. Or would they think she was dishonest? After all, she'd been hiding Olivia and Ben in her house for months before they knew. She had imagined herself in prison and had watched a couple of episodes of *Orange is the New Black*. A bad idea as it sent her perception of ladies' prisons into thinking that she would have no choice but to go down on women while they cornrowed her hair. Orange did nothing for her complexion, either.

Jane was trying to be calm for Olivia's sake more than anything. But when Julian came to collect Ben to sleep over at his house tonight, she could see the panic creeping through Olivia's body like a rampant virus. She was kissing her son like he was never returning, and Jane realised that this was probably the first time Ben had not been with her overnight. While not wanting to make a big deal of it, Jane made a point of saying to Ben that he would have lots of fun, and when he came back, he had to help her plant some flowers for the garden. She tried to make it all seem totally natural, and to Ben, it was; that was the main thing.

Olivia was upstairs, also looking out for a car pulling up. She was in the small room at the front of the house, which for the last three months had been Ben's room. It was much smaller than his old bedroom in Lyndhurst, but he still had everything he needed around him. Olivia would sleep in his bed tonight so Jeff could take the double in her room. It seemed strange to call it 'her room', but it was, and she realised that it was the most comfortable room she'd ever been in because it was in a house where she felt unconditional love.

If she hadn't knocked on Jane's door back in December, where would she be now? Would she have gone back to Derek? She hated to think she would have been that weak, but part of her knew she probably would have returned to the miserable existence she'd encouraged so many years ago. What a fool she'd been to believe Derek's lies and to allow him to invade so much of her being. He was there at work and at home. Even the little amusement she had in her life was with him, as she had no friends. She had naively thought all she needed was him, but when Ben came along, she suspected he had cheated on her as he had with Jane.

With a bit of digging around, she'd found out about the other women, including Demi, who had allowed him to cheat and lie about the business. There were others, but after a couple of years, she resigned herself to the fact that all she needed was Ben, a roof over their heads, and to keep her trap shut. She'd been treated the same as Jane, but the only difference was when Jane found out, she was strong enough to go it alone, and Olivia had always admired her for that. Jane had some funny ways and, in some respects, was the biggest snob of them all, but after everything she'd put up with, even from the early years of Derek's mother, wasn't she allowed to be a snob? Wasn't she allowed to have standards? Olivia only wished that she would be like Jane one day.

Olivia's and Jane's thoughts were simultaneously interrupted as the silver BMW pulled up outside the house. Olivia ran halfway down the stairs but stopped when she saw Jane at the bottom, reaching for the front door. As Jane stepped outside, Olivia could hear her whooping and sounding grateful about something. She wanted to move but was rooted to the spot and concluded she was quite happy to stay there until circumstances said she needed to move.

Jane walked in with a blonde woman behind her of similar age to Jane. She looked up at Olivia on the stairs.

"You must be Olivia." The woman smiled, and even though she was a stranger, Olivia felt love in that smile.

A man bustled in behind the women carrying a couple of holdall-type bags and a plastic bag that clanked with the unmistakable sound of bottles, shoulder rubbing with their, no doubt, welcomed content. The man looked at Olivia and gave her a warm smile, and as she smiled back at him, she felt relief. In one look, he seemed to say, *I'm here. It'll be all right. I've got you,* and she knew she was safe.

"Olivia, this is Daisy, and this is Jeff. I didn't know Daisy was coming!" Jane seemed flustered. The extra visitor had clearly taken her by surprise.

"Hello, Olivia," Jeff and Daisy spoke in unison. By the time Olivia realised she had bound down the last half of the stairs, she was already being hugged by Daisy.

"I'm so glad you agreed to come," gushed Olivia.

"You knew?" asked Jane.

Olivia nodded with a broad grin.

"Any chance of a cuppa?" asked Jeff.

"Yes! Yes! Come through. I'll put the kettle on. Olivia, can you take those bags up to your room?" Jane picked up the clanking bag. "I take it this lot is for the fridge?" she asked with a smirk.

After putting the bags and wine away, the kettle was boiled, and everyone returned to the kitchen and sat around the table. Jeff began talking of the journey down and how he hadn't been to this part of the south coast before. He talked of Cornwall, Devon and Dorset and how much he liked them.

"Those counties get most of the tourist trade, but we still have beautiful spots in our county, too," said Jane as she placed a big pot of tea in the centre of the table.

They drank the tea and refilled the pot while they all spoke at a hundred miles an hour about everything they could think of. Once the tea was finished, Olivia admitted she fancied a glass of wine, and they all cheered at the suggestion.

Over the next few hours, the conversation became less animated, as if they knew they had to talk about the thing they'd been avoiding all afternoon. It was Jane who took the first tentative step.

"So, Daisy, as happy as I am to see you, I'm wondering why you're here. Have you come just to see me and keep Jeff company in the car?"

"Well, you got two out of three," said Daisy.

"I suspected there was another reason."

"Before we go into the ins and outs, can I suggest we get something to eat before our bellies are full of wine?" said Jeff. "There are a few things we need to discuss, and we need to get this right."

"Absolutely!" Jane jumped to her feet and was soon turning dials on the oven to make ready for her pre-prepared lasagne, which had been cooked that morning. She was glad, not knowing what Jeff's appetite was like, that she'd made a large portion. She could always make a bowl of salad too.

"Jane, is it okay if I take these two ladies through to the lounge?" asked Jeff. "There are a couple of things we need to go over."

"Of course." She walked to the lounge to check that everything was perfect for them and was soon followed by her guests.

"Thanks, Jane." Jeff gave her a look that expected her to leave. He picked up on her confusion as she continued to stare at him. "You and I will chat once I've finished with the girls." His tone had an air of finality about it, and Jane took the cue to leave.

When she returned to the kitchen, the atmosphere felt flat. Her anxiety began to creep back into the pit of her stomach and her head began to whirl. She couldn't understand how she could be involved. Was Jeff simply just looking after Olivia? Surely, Daisy would have her back. But Daisy admitted that Jeff had told her very little. However, she must know something; otherwise, why would she be here? And why did Jeff need her? Daisy didn't know Olivia or Derek.

Then another thought popped into her head. Did she know Daisy? It wasn't as if they were lifelong friends who'd witnessed each other's weddings and watched their children grow up. She wasn't there when Derek left her; when she'd thought her world had ended. What if she had Daisy all wrong? Was it fair to say that Daisy was nothing more than a pen pal?

She realised that her thoughts were rampaging out of control and reached for a glass of Prosecco. *That won't help,* she thought to herself, and before she knew it, her mobile was in her hand and she was dialling Dominic's number. She was climbing the stairs and heading for her bedroom when he answered. He was bright and cheery, and she hesitated whether to confide in him. She'd told him everything, and he was a great listener, even raising details she had missed simply to make her feel better.

After the usual pleasantries, Dominic asked if Jeff had arrived and when she said that Daisy had come too, he seemed surprised, which heightened when Jane said she didn't know she was coming until they pulled up.

"Maybe she wanted to come to give you some support?"

"No, it's not just that. Jeff wants to talk to me about something, and he's having a discussion in the lounge with Olivia *and* Daisy. Why does he need Daisy? It doesn't make sense."

"Do they plan to tell you?"

"Yes."

"Then stop fretting. Cook your lasagne, set the table and take a breath. You're filling in lots of blanks, probably incorrectly, when all you need to do is wait an hour or two and they'll tell you. I'm sure they're not keeping things from you on purpose."

"How do you know?"

"Well, they wouldn't bloody sit in your lounge to conspire against you, would they? They'd have some clandestine meeting in an underground car park like they do on the telly—all wearing trench coats and carrying briefcases while they talk about how they're going to bring down the middle-aged divorcee who volunteers for the Harvest Festival and kills bonsai trees."

She laughed, and each chuckle released her tension. She knew she was being ridiculous; she'd just needed someone to tell her so her thoughts could get back on track.

"Feel better, darling?"

He'd called her darling, and she smiled. It was natural.

"I do."

"Call me later."

"I will. Bye."

She was glad she'd called him and knew he probably would be happy that he was the one she'd reached out to.

As she went down the stairs, Jane looked at her watch and wondered how much longer they would be. As she entered the kitchen, the smell from her oven told her that dinner was ready. Should she disturb them? She didn't want it to burn. She'd gone to the farm shop to get her groceries for this weekend and had gasped a little at the total price when she'd only filled one shopping bag, but there was no denying the quality was there.

As she pulled her best Le Creuset dish from the oven, she shouted out to them that it was on the table, and by the time she'd replaced all the wine glasses with fresh ones, they were filing in with hungry smiles.

"I love lasagne," admitted Daisy. "It's so nice to have someone cook for me for a change."

"I took you out last night!" exclaimed Jeff.

"That's not the same. It's not a home-cooked meal. Home food tastes different to restaurant food."

"It's true that. I wonder why that is," mused Olivia.

"Because restaurant food is made with precision, but home food is made with love." Olivia loved Daisy's explanation and hoped she could repeat it herself one day.

There were lots of compliments about Jane's cooking, which she believed when she cleared the four empty plates. It was worth the small fortune she'd paid, knowing none of it went to waste.

"There's Eton Mess for dessert, which Ben helped with. To be honest, he did most of it, bless him. He's such a great help."

"He was so excited to learn how to make meringue and hold the bowl over his head," said Olivia.

"He may grow up to be a budding chef one day. He loves all the cookery programmes—*MasterChef, Saturday Kitchen*—but his favourite is *Bake Off*."

"I should get our Cheryl to watch a cookery programme," said Daisy. "I once asked her if the kids would like quesadillas, and she replied, 'They only wear Adidas.'" She shrugged while the others giggled.

Ben's Eton Mess went down as well as the first course, and after much scraping of bowls, Jeff helped Jane load the dishwasher.

"We'll wipe the tops down, won't we, Oliva? You two go in the lounge, and we'll finish off." Daisy was ushering Jane and Jeff out. She knew Jane would be on pins, especially as they had been talking earlier without her there.

Jane swiped her recently filled glass of Prosecco and followed Jeff into the lounge. Daisy noticed that she was walking stiffly, a clear indication that she was far from relaxed, but she knew that once Jeff had spoken to her, she would be fine. Jeff had a voice that soothed people. When she first met him, she thought his voice was sexy and slow, and while she still thought that, she also realised that it was comforting and calming. His Liverpudlian accent was obvious but not harsh as she had heard from some people on the telly. She liked the way he talked.

Daisy sat at the table while Olivia popped things into cupboards. It was clear the woman had lived here a while, as she subconsciously tidied away, still talking to Daisy. Daisy watched her and studied her form. She was beautiful, there was no getting away from that, and her hourglass figure was to die for. She'd only seen pictures of Derek and knew he wasn't the most attractive chocolate in the box, so whatever did she see in him?

Daisy thought on the journey down that it was likely she would dislike Olivia. She thought it wrong that this woman had landed on her friend's doorstep and taken advantage of her good nature. But in the short time she had known her, and from what little Jeff could say, Daisy was confident this woman was just like the rest of them—insecure, scared, lonely and needing someone to listen to her and guide her with her choices in life. Yes, she was just like her and Jane.

"Have you met Dominic?" asked Daisy.

"Oh yes. He's been here a few times. He's ever so nice. I think it was one-sided for a while, with him being keener, but lately, she's starting to like him more. He popped in the other day to ask her to lunch, and she jumped at the chance. A few months ago, I think he would have struggled to step over the threshold. But he's good for her, and he's being really patient, and you can see he adores her."

Olivia had finished cleaning and sat at the table opposite Daisy. She liked this woman and wished she had a friend like that in her life. Olivia used to think she would be whole if she had a man by her side, but as she gotten older, she'd realised what she actually needed was a friend. Jane was proving to be the best she had, but she knew Jane would never feel like that about her. She was the one who caused the marriage to break up, not intentionally, but she was aware that Derek had a wife from the word go, and she'd still pursued him. Jane had recently said she had forgiven her, but Olivia would never forgive herself.

"She'll miss you when you leave. And Ben."

"I'm hoping I'll still see her every day!"

"If she goes for the plan."

"I can't do it without her, Daisy."

"You can. Yes, it will be harder, but we have to respect her decision at the end of the day."

"I worry about how Julian will take it all."

"You leave Julian to his mother. He's her problem. But I suspect Julian has grown up since Myla was born and understands what a parent is and what family means, so I wouldn't worry too much about him."

They chatted more about their lives, and Daisy told Olivia about James, her dad, Cheryl and the grandkids while Olivia gave a potted history of her parents, living in Jersey and her job in Derek's firm.

"Being unpopular because I was sleeping with the boss meant I moved departments a lot. There isn't a department that I haven't worked in." Olivia looked sad. "You'd think after all that I would have made one friend."

"Maybe you were a snooty bitch." Daisy gave it straight, and Olivia was a little shocked at the statement but within a few seconds saw her whole career flash before her.

"You know what, Daisy? You're right. I was actually a complete cow. I've been blaming my relationship with Derek for having no friends, but all the time, it was me. I've been awful to some people. Lording it over them because I was sleeping with the boss."

"Well, you're not sleeping with him anymore, and now you know that maybe you could have been a bit nicer to people.

Lessons learned and all that. And what's all this about not having friends? What the hell is Jane? And I know we've just met, but I'd like to think that we could be proper friends too. Jeff likes you, so you can't be that bad."

"I hope we become proper friends."

Daisy reached out for Olivia's hand and gave it a maternal pat. She was about to suggest they open another bottle of Prosecco when they heard the lounge door open. Both ladies raised their eyebrows and waited for Jane to enter. Jeff walked in first, but his face was relaxed, giving nothing away. However, when Jane walked in, she looked amused.

"What are you smirking at?" asked Daisy.

"I'm not smirking."

"You look like you've taken a secret shit somewhere and got away with it."

Jane burst out laughing, and Daisy turned to Jeff.

"So are we on then?"

"Let's do it!"

Friday, 23rd April

Olivia was the first to rise. She'd hardly slept due to a combination of nerves and sleeping in her son's single bed. She had her shower in the downstairs wet room instead of the main bathroom upstairs so she wouldn't wake anyone. By half six, she had her make-up on and was waiting for the house to stir to life before using her hairdryer.

It was ten to seven when she heard the first person rise and use the toilet. The unmistakable sound of someone relieving themselves from a height told her it was a man. If Jeff was up, she could presume that Daisy would not be far behind him. She was about to start drying her hair when there was a knock. Jane poked her around the door, armed with a cup of tea.

"I made this for you." She placed it on Ben's desk, which was now serving as his mother's dressing table. "You were up early."

"I'm sorry! Did I wake you?"

"You'd have to be asleep first to be woken up."

"I didn't sleep much either."

"Do you want something to eat?"

"No, thanks. I feel a bit sick."

"A bit! My stomach feels like a washing machine. I might need to take some Kalms before we go. You dry your hair, and I'll meet you downstairs."

"Thanks, Jane."

Jane walked back to her bedroom. She had already showered in her en suite but still needed to put on her make-up. She looked at the black Reiss dress laid across her bed. It was formal, conservative and what people expected, but something told her the dress wasn't quite right. She scolded herself for being vain when her thoughts should be focused on how today would go. Sometimes when she thought of it, she felt a little sad. How had it come to this? But then she would answer the question by answering that Derek had brought all of this on himself, and they were simply taking advantage of it, just like he had with her and Olivia for years.

She sat at the dressing table and looked at her reflection. Sometimes she looked at herself and quite liked the woman who looked back at her, but today she wasn't sure. She looked old today. Was it any wonder Derek left her for the voluptuous Olivia? She had developed her look over the years with plenty of steering from Derek. *"You shouldn't eat that…" "You need to eat this…" "You can't wear that…" "You're not thirty anymore…" "Why are you wearing make-up?"* The list went on.

She dug around the drawer, looking for a particular bra, and thought of all the times she'd done as she was told. Derek's mother had been the same with him, and then he copied the same behaviour with Jane. She had resisted things early in the marriage and was even sometimes rebellious, but as the years went by, she didn't have the strength to argue with him anymore, and before she knew it, his opinion was her opinion. She laughed at how much she had allowed him to manipulate her and the fact that she didn't even notice it in the later years. She'd learned to conform and be the perfect wife, but he'd still left her.

By half eight, Jeff, Daisy and Olivia were ready and waiting for Jane in the kitchen. Jeff kept looking at his watch.

"What time are we meeting Brendan?" asked Daisy as she glanced at the kitchen clock.

"A quarter to nine," replied Jeff, "but that's at the coffee place."

"Neil's just texted to say he's already there," said Olivia as she turned off her phone and put in her small Mulberry handbag. She'd picked out a grey, tailored, pencil-skirt dress to wear today. With a burgundy belt to cinch in her waist and her handbag of a similar shade, it made sense to wear the same colour stiletto shoes. She felt smart, businesslike, and the outfit gave her confidence.

"Give her a knock, will you, Daisy," asked Jeff.

Daisy was about to do as she was asked when they heard Jane coming down the stairs. Jeff grabbed his car keys from the kitchen counter, and Daisy fetched her handbag when she heard Olivia gasp. Daisy turned to look at Jane and heard a "Wow!" come from Jeff.

"I was going to wear the black dress, but then I thought sod it!"

Jane stood in the kitchen in a siren-red trouser suit. The single-breasted jacket was buttoned with the only button it possessed, and a white silk camisole peaked just above it. Her nude court shoes were high, and she towered over all of them; her face, usually bare-skinned, was covered in expertly applied make-up. She looked ten years younger.

"You look great, Jane, but…er…we need to go." Jeff, being a typical man, didn't feel she needed any more compliments than that. If she were his woman, then of course, he would gush more, but she wasn't, and they didn't have time to critique her outfit choice.

"You look incredible," whispered Daisy in her ear as she hugged her with approval. Daisy followed Jeff to the car while Olivia rummaged in her handbag. Jane waited at the end of the hall for her so she could lock the door behind her, but as Olivia approached, she raised the small make-up item in her hand and passed it to Jane. It was a lipstick. Jane, a little confused, took it from Olivia.

"If you're going to do this, then do it properly," said Olivia.

Jane turned to face the small mirror hanging by the front door. She pulled the top off the gold-encased stick of scarlet and smeared it over her lips. The colour was pure red, and with every swipe, she could feel herself changing into the woman she was before Derek had eroded her. Confidence was soaring through her, and her nerves were turning to steel. Olivia stood behind her and watched her apply it like she had been wearing it all her life, and after popping the lid back on, Jane slowly handed it back.

"Let's get the bastard."

***

The coffee shop was over the road from Hubbard Consultants & Contractors, and when the four of them entered, they caught the attention of most of the clientele waiting for their morning fix. Olivia spotted Neil, Derek's old accountant, straight away. He looked happy to see her but extremely nervous.

"How many coffees has he had? He's sweating like a Jew at a Catholic mass," whispered Daisy to Jane.

"Olivia makes him nervous. He fancies the pants off her."

"Well, he's gonna blow a gasket when he cops an eyeful of you." Daisy and Jane giggled in the queue like a couple of schoolgirls.

"What can I get you?" asked the barista.

"Three flat whites and a latte for Christie Brinkley here." The joke was lost on the eighteen-year-old.

"Anything else?"

"What about Neil?" asked Jane.

"And half a dozen napkins for the puddle talking at table ten," said Daisy with a straight face. Jane smiled, glad Daisy was here with her today.

By the time the women walked over to the group, another man had walked in and was heading straight for them. Jeff recognised him and smiled.

"Sorry, mate. Been driving round for ages trying to dump the car somewhere."

"Don't worry. We've just got here ourselves," said Jeff as he shook the man's hand. "Everybody, this is Brendan, who I was telling you about. Brendan, this is Olivia, Jane, Neil, who was Derek's accountant, and this is Daisy, my girlfriend, but she's here today in a professional capacity."

"Ya bird?" Brendan smirked at Jeff.

"Me bird," said Jeff trying not to laugh too much.

"Hiya, love. He's told me all about you. Not being funny, though, you could do miles better than him." He winked at Daisy, who looked at a blushing Jeff. "Right, who wants a coffee?"

"Just sort yourself out," said Jeff.

Brendan was dressed in a sharp, mid-blue suit, and his shirt and tie were immaculate. His shoes looked expensive, and he smelled divine.

"How long have you known Brendan?" asked Olivia as she watched him being served.

"I went to school with him, and then we went to the same university. He studied law and I did accountancy."

"Does he still live in Liverpool?" asked Daisy.

"No. He lives in London. Has done for a few years. Met a girl from Sierra Leone, and they've been married for about twenty years, I think. His eldest is in Liverpool Uni, though, so I get to see Brendan a bit more now."

"London? He sounds expensive," said Neil.

"He owes me a pint, so stop worrying."

"Yeah, calm down. I'm not sure they have any more napkins left," snipped Daisy as she watched Neil wipe his brow for the hundredth time.

Brendan soon returned and took the last empty chair at the table.

"We all set then?" asked Brendan.

"We think so. What we're doing is fairly straightforward. It's just his reaction we can't be sure of," answered Jeff.

"He'll fight," Jane said.

"We quite like a scrap, don't we, Jeff?" joked Brendan.

They continued to sip their coffee and talk over the finer details, which were peppered with humour. Brendan was a welcome addition, and his wit and wisecracks made the atmosphere a lot lighter. Even Neil was beginning to relax. But it was short-lived when he did a little jump in his seat.

"There he is!"

They all looked over to where Neil was pointing, and they could see Derek walking into the building. He stopped briefly at the reception desk that was still visible from inside the coffee shop. Then, after being passed a bundle of mail, he made his way to the lift behind the reception desk.

"Let's give him a minute to open up his railway magazine and Viagra subscription forms," suggested Jane. "I'm off to the ladies'."

Jane walked into the ladies' toilet at the far end of the coffee shop, and after locking the door, she pressed her back against it and took a large breath. In her mind, she could hear a voice telling her to be calm and that she was strong. She walked over to the poorly lit mirror to check her make-up. Even in the grim, grey light, she knew she looked great. Then, after an encouraging smile, she washed and dried her hands even though she hadn't used the toilet.

When she walked out, she could see them all waiting for her. Daisy looked a little nervous, while Olivia looked different too. She looked confident. No, not confident. Cocky. Jane knew her enough now to know it was all an act. That slight look of disdain on Olivia's face made the group look more assertive.

They filed out of the coffee shop and were soon following in Derek's footsteps. They entered Hubbard Consultants & Contractors, with Olivia leading the way.

"Hi, Olivia," said the confused receptionist as she looked at the rest of the party. "I didn't know we were having visitors today."

"Well, I guess you don't know everything then, do you, Amy?"

The receptionist visibly shrank in her swivel chair.

Olivia continued to walk to the lift and shouted to the receptionist, "Please hold all calls to Mr Hubbard until further instruction. We are not to be disturbed under any circumstances."

The lift immediately opened as soon as Olivia pressed the button, and she stood back to allow them all to enter. Jane was the last and stepped in with Olivia. The door shut, and the lift began to ascend.

"I'm walking in first," said Jane. No one argued.

The lift doors opened, revealing a brightly lit, open-plan office. As soon as Jane stepped onto the floor, every head seemed to turn and watch the group confidently stride towards Derek's office at the far end of the floor. The buzz grew quieter and quieter as they neared the glass office, where they could see Derek sitting at his desk.

They were only a few yards away when he saw the lady in red leading a group towards him. He then saw Olivia and Neil with faces he didn't recognise. By the time he realised the scarlet-clad woman was Jane, she was turning the handle to his door.

"Derek," she gushed. Her voice was strong and assured. "You remember Neil, don't you?" She waved her hand in his direction. "And this is Daisy, my darling friend, and this is Jeff, her gorgeous boyfriend, who is also an accountant—like you, Neil." Like Neil had just learned of this fact. "And this is Brendan." She purposely didn't reveal his occupation. "And, of course, you know Olivia. Mother of your child, Ben. Darling Ben."

Derek was on his feet.

"You know as much about Ben as I do of this rabble that you've brought in here. I'm busy, Jane. So take your new yoga chums and get out. Preferably to a sink to wash all that crap off your face." He began laughing at his own joke, which stopped when no one moved.

"Let me get this right," said Brendan. "You were married to him?" He turned to Olivia. "And you gave him a kid?" He shifted his gaze between them.

Both women smiled and nodded.

"A bloody Scouser," hissed Derek.

"Make that two," added Jeff.

"And I'm from Chorley," drawled Daisy.

"Has someone shut the North? What the hell are you all doing in my office?"

"Sit down, Derek. I want to tell you a story," said Jane.

He went to argue, and she raised an eyebrow. He didn't know she could do that. When he sat down, Olivia and Jane took the seats on the opposite side of his desk. Daisy sat on the small couch behind them, and Neil sat beside her. Brendan casually sat on the couch's arm while Jeff remained standing with his back to the door.

"Once upon a time," started Jane, "there was a young girl called Jane who fell in love with a toad called Derek. With a dream in their heart, they created a small company called Hubbard Consultants & Contractors from their spare room in their first house not ten miles away from here. They beavered away for a couple of years, and realising they needed staff, they rented some office space on the ground floor of this very building. The business grew, and so did their staff. More importantly, so did their bank balance. They bought a beautiful house and started a family. With the business growing, they also bought the building they were previously renting. Jane was helping the staff move their desks into this lovely space when her waters broke.

"Now, unfortunately, Jane didn't come back to the business for five whole years, and a lot changed in that time. But Jane was happy again. Her son had started school, and for some reason she can't fathom, she was happy that she could see more of the toad, as together they rubbed along, building the business until one day, it seemed that Jane had enough. Maybe it was a mid-life crisis, or maybe she wanted to do something for herself, so she left. But Jane never did do something for herself. Instead, she created a beautiful home for her son and the toad while her ambitions were slowly cooked and cleaned away.

"She did toy with the idea of returning, but the toad insisted that his new help was doing a splendid job looking after the business. Eight years later, nearly two years ago, Jane realised that the new help was also looking after the toad, and that's where the story changes. Well, two stories—actually three, all running parallel to each other.

"Jane's story is of devastation. Her beautiful son had already left home. The home she'd created for her family had now all gone. What was she to do? She would lose everything. She had no job, no husband and now probably no home. She decided she needed help to see if she could claim half of the business at least. But the toad took pity on poor Jane and said, 'Fret no more, Princess. Take the house that you love, and I will take the business you walked away from.' She deliberated, and with bad advice from a lawyer who was the toad's friend, she accepted the offer. With a little deposit in her bank account each month, she could live quite happily once she'd mended her broken heart."

The room was captivated by her story. Daisy was so proud of her friend, and she watched in awe as Jane remained steeled as Derek sniffed and sneered throughout.

"Princess Jane's story doesn't end there, though. It soon became apparent from a rhododendron bush that the toad and the help were now living together and had been for years. And not only that, they had a son. A son called Ben. Princess Jane, of course, was shocked. Who wouldn't be? But soon, she came to terms with the fact that the toad was no longer hers, and she was glad.

"And that should be the end of Princess Jane's story, but here she still is, sitting in front of the toad."

"I haven't got time for fairy tales," growled Derek.

"This is no fairy tale."

"Then get to the point!"

Jane took a slow and deliberate breath and rested her hands on her tummy as she sat back and crossed her long legs.

"Once upon a time, there was a toad called Derek. He was brilliant at starting and growing a business with his princess wife called Jane. He was also brilliant at manipulation, duplicity, lying, deception, greed and betrayal."

Derek was no longer smiling. Surely, they didn't know…

"One day, the toad decided he didn't want to be with the princess anymore and told her she could stay in the castle. But unbeknown to Princess Jane, the toad had bought another castle. This one was even bigger and better, and the new help also became a princess.

"But Princess Olivia wasn't happy. She realised the toad was actually just a toad, and like Princess Jane before her, she kept the house beautiful. But because the house was so big, the toad hired help, so Princess Olivia returned to rule over the kingdom of Hubbard Consultants & Contractors with the toad. But Princess Olivia still wasn't happy. No one in the kingdom liked her very much, and why? Well, she was fucking a toad, that's why. But the ironic thing was she wasn't fucking the toad. The toad was boring. The toad was old. And soon, her dreams of escaping became a reality just before Christmas. A mere four months ago. Princess Olivia took her son the day before Christmas Eve and celebrated the biggest day of the year with a McDonald's burger in a local inn called the Travelodge.

"Poor Princess Olivia. Where could she go? Who did she know? No one liked her, and no one would understand. Except for one person. Princess Jane! A couple of days after Christmas Day, Olivia begged Jane for help, and out of the goodness of her heart, Jane opened the door to her castle for Olivia and Ben."

Derek sat up straight and stared at Olivia. "You're telling me that you went to her for help, and she let you stay the night? Give over."

"It was more than a night," said Olivia.

"How long?"

"Did you put the dishwasher on this morning before we left?" Jane asked Olivia.

"You're still there!!"

"And that's more or less the end of Princess Olivia's story." Jane sniffed and swept away invisible lint from her thigh.

"So that's what all this is about. You came here to tell me that you two live together? And what are these lot here for? Or has she moved you all in as well and started a commune for lost Northerners?"

"Oh, I like that idea," said Daisy and shifted to face Jeff. "What d'you reckon?"

"It depends on where the commune is going to be. I mean, is it in castle number one or castle number two in Lyndhurst."

"That house is mine!" spat Derek. Jeff stepped forward, placed his knuckles face down on Derek's desk, and leaned on them to get closer to Derek.

"Technically, it's not. It belongs to the business. Olivia always believed that the house belonged to you, but after a bit of digging after a reliable tip-off…"

Derek shot Neil a venomous look.

"…we discovered that the deeds for the house are owned by Hubbard Consultants & Contractors."

"So? It's my business." How much had Neil told them?

"Again, technically, it's not." Jeff was using his soft and sensual voice, which made the scene look more sinister than it actually was.

Derek realised that Neil had said too much.

"It's transferring back now if that's what you're talking about."

"You mean the sale of the business back to yourself? Because at the moment, it belongs to Olivia."

"I only did it so she couldn't get her hands on it." Derek jabbed a finger in Jane's direction. "The business was always mine. So I fiddled a sale because of a divorce. Big deal. She got what she wanted, and she's happy now, living like Thelma & Louise with my ex in a house that I bloody paid for."

"With a business that I helped start and grow," said Jane.

"You're carrying on like you had nothing. I gave you everything!"

"Well, again, technically, you didn't," said Jeff.

"What do you want? Money? I'll write you a cheque now. Name your price, and let's bring an end to this crap version of *This is Your Life*! But if you think you are getting your hands on the business, forget it."

"Who's putting this sale through? Your solicitor?"

"The papers are being finalised today."

"So you forged Olivia's signature again?"

"Yes, but it's not like I stole from her. This was never hers. Jane might have a point, but Olivia doesn't. Anyway, it's done now."

"It certainly is," said Jeff.

Jeff turned to face Brendan, who was digging in his briefcase for a file he passed to Jeff. Derek eyed the file suspiciously and slightly retreated when Jeff slid it towards him.

"These are copies of documents signed yesterday showing that Olivia Martin, the sole owner of Hubbard Consultants

& Contractors, agreed to the sale, which was concluded yesterday and filed in London."

Derek went to speak, but no words came out.

"I'd like to clarify," said Brendan, who was still sitting on the arm of the chair like he was about to burst into an Irish song, "that the house was not part of the sale. Hubbard Consultants & Contractors sold the house to Olivia Martin."

"So, who bought my company?"

"I did." Daisy stood up and smiled at him. "Cost me a whole pound."

"You can't do this! I'll take you to court and say it was a revenge sale. When I show them the books, they'll see that the business is worth over a million." Derek's mouth was becoming drier. He lifted his coffee cup, hoping there would be a tiny drop, but it was empty.

"Which books would they be?" asked Neil.

"You traitorous bastard. After all I did for you!"

"Me! You did nothing for me except haggle about my rates and threaten me whenever I said I wanted out. I made more money from doing the books for the butcher in Market Square." This was the first time Neil had stood up to Derek. Finally, he could put the bully in his place.

"Well, what the hell are you going to do with the business? I look out there and don't see people. I see mortgages and bills and nursery fees. I'm responsible for all that! No offence, love, but you look like you'd struggle to balance your Lloyds housekeeping account."

"I'm offended! I bank with Santander." Daisy stepped forward and placed her hands on Jane's shoulders. "We feel that until all this is settled and you hop back to the pond you grew from, the business can stay in my name. I'll be appointing Jane and Olivia as joint directors while I stay a silent owner. I've no marriage or blood connection, and any court in the land will see I've bought this company in good faith."

"For a fucking pound!" Derek was apoplectic with rage.

"I know! What a bargain! Especially when I heard that Olivia bought the house for…how much?" asked Daisy.

"Two pounds. I didn't have a pound coin."

"You're not going to get away with this," spat Derek.

"I think they will, mate," said Brendan. "Your accountant here furnished us with the real books—no wonder you're pissed off that the business was sold for a pound. Profits for the last year alone are in excess of six hundred thousand, but when I checked with Companies House, it seems you only declared a profit of ninety. So where did over five hundred grand go? Er…where was it? Oh, I know! Fantasy Island!"

"Cayman Islands," said Neil.

"Oh aye, yeah, the Cayman Islands. Very nice it is there too. Took the missus a couple of years back, but I was disappointed that no one was shouting 'The plane! The plane!' when we landed. Still, they make a decent mojito. But I digress. As a lawyer, I can say that all the transactions that have taken place are above board, and I even have a record of the payment taking place."

He pulled out his phone and started scrolling, then found a photo of a hand with a pound resting in its palm. Brendan pushed the phone in Derek's direction with a huge grin on his face. "That's not my hand. That's his." He pointed at Jeff. "He's an accountant as well, so I'm pretty sure that the sums are right. It's a shame you didn't have him do your books instead of this sweat over here."

Neil hung his head, aware that his clothes were damp.

"So by all means, mate, get your lawyer involved once he's put this imaginary sale through today and finished spinning straw into gold in your stationery cupboard. We've got all the documents for him." Brendan retrieved his suitcase and started throwing files onto Derek's desk. "The original forged documents that Olivia had no knowledge of. The deeds of the house in the business name. The Cayman Islands bank account. The accounts, including profit and loss, for the last ten years for the company, both sets, the real ones and the not-so-real ones. And there's you kidding on you don't like fairy tales when these numbers are a work of fiction. I've also got this little memory stick." He waved it before throwing it on top of the pile. "Every invoice for non-existent contractors you paid into accounts in the Cayman Islands is on there."

Brendan walked around the desk until he was on the same side as Derek and perched in front of him. Then, grabbing both arms of Derek's chair, he pushed his face inches from Derek's. "We found all this in a few weeks. Imagine what else we'd find if we kept looking. Any more Demis out there? Shall we go out there and ask who else is on the fiddle? Yeah, we've even got the records showing you paying her off each month to keep her trap shut."

"What do you want from me?" Derek croaked.

"Girls?" Brendan's tone was bright and cheery.

"I want you out of the house by Sunday," said Olivia. "Take the cars, your clothes and your bloody trains."

"Where do I go?" he simpered.

"Somewhere you can't be found. These women have no choice but to blow you up to keep themselves clean," said Brendan.

"Jane?" He looked at her imploringly. "Julian? Myla?"

"That's the bit that breaks my heart. How you deal with them is up to you. You have until Sunday to see them."

"Ben?" he asked Olivia.

"Don't act like you care. You didn't even know where he was living until half an hour ago."

"I need money to leave."

"Remember the old account we had for holidays?" said Jane. "Well, Olivia and I have left money in it for you. There's enough there to set you up somewhere very far away."

"And are you going to run this with the vicar? I mean seriously. A vicar?!"

"If the angels wanted us to end up with men like you, they would never have invented good men. *Like the vicar.*" Jane smiled. She'd always hated his angel excuses. Finally, she could fire one back. It would be the last.

Derek was cornered. He knew that if he fought, he would end up with a massive fine, possibly a jail sentence. He could probably take Jane and Olivia on, but these Scousers knew what they were talking about. He often wondered if he'd done the right thing getting rid of Neil. Clearly, he'd underestimated him. And Demi? He'd agreed to her blackmailing demands, and still she'd blabbed. Was there no loyalty left in the world? He had no choice.

Who would have thought that today was the day his life would change? He'd known when he started fiddling that it couldn't last forever, but he did think that it would be him that brought an end to it all. He never thought it would be his exes—especially Jane. He looked at her, and she reminded him of when they first met. She was feisty and full of life, but then she'd changed, and he'd become bored of her. If she'd stayed like the old Jane, none of this would have happened. He wouldn't have had to go seeking comfort elsewhere, and because of that, he was forced to cook the books to keep them both happy. It was all her fault.

He'd had no choice.

With one last look at Olivia, he grabbed his coat from the stand and opened the door. The buzz of the office continued, as they were used to the visitors now. Derek would often leave at all times of the day, so no one paid him any attention as he left for the last time. They didn't notice the defeated man walking into the lift. They also didn't notice how quickly he changed and the look of defiance when he left the lift and walked straight past the reception.

He quickly pulled out his phone, logged on to an app and was relieved to see a particular bank account balance was still intact and very healthy. With a huge grin, he did a quick search and found a number. After three short rings, he was connected.

"Hi. Can you tell me the times of flights from Gatwick to Hong Kong either today or tomorrow?"

He reached his car, already making a mental list. Home for some personal belongings and then into Southampton to get a new phone and empty the old holiday account. God knows how much they'd put in there. He wasn't expecting much, but he felt more than comfortable with the balance in the Hong Kong account.

"There's a flight this evening from Gatwick at 11:20 p.m."

He thought of Julian. He could leave a note. *That would be okay. It would be easier too. Yes, that would be fine.*

"Can you hold it for me for a half hour? I'm shooting home to get my passport." The Triumph TR3 disappeared as it headed towards Lyndhurst.

Derek found his passport but forgot to look for note paper.

He remembered the forgotten note somewhere over Germany.

Later that year...

To: jane-hubbard@skycorres.co.uk

From: daisyduke71@gomail.com

Date: **Friday, 31ˢᵗ December 18:30**

Dear Jane

I'm sending you this email while I'm waiting for my hair to be done. Our Cheryl bought me a set of rollers for Christmas. Her mate's mum got a set last year, and her hair is always lovely, so I'm hoping for the same results.

How're things going? Was it lovely having Myla for her first Christmas? I bet you ruined her. The photos you attached on your last email were beautiful. Olivia did the house up lovely. How many trees did she have? I lost count! I don't know where she finds the time with running the business. She's like a superwoman.

As I said in my email last month, Jeff and I are off to a New Year's Eve Ball in Didsbury. I hope I don't bump into Dean. Can you imagine? Jade said he's still single, so I can't imagine him wanting to go somewhere like that on his own. I'm really looking forward to it, and we're staying in the hotel where the ball is being held, so we don't have far to stagger to bed.

The sale of my house should be completed by the end of Jan, so I need to start packing things up now. Thanks again for all your top tips these last few months. I've done as you said and thrown an awful lot of things away. I didn't realise how many of James's things I still had. Cheryl took some of them, but the rest went to the charity shop or was binned. I thought I would find it hard, but it felt right to do it. I also did the same with Dad's stuff. Like you said last summer, it's only stuff. Why am I holding on to it?

Cheryl said she would help me next weekend and bring our Bruno, as he can bubble wrap all the little bits. I still can't believe how supportive she's being. Thank goodness she gets on with Jeff, but who doesn't? And she completely understands about me buying a house in Cheshire with him. It makes sense. It's not too far away from everybody but far enough to not have Cheryl dumping the kids every weekend. Kelvin is still working for the council and loves it. Who knew being a bin man could bring so much satisfaction?

Anyway, once we're settled in the house, you should all come up and stay with us. Our Bruno still talks about Ben and wants to know when he'll see him again. They had such a lovely time last August, didn't they?

Did you manage to grab a few hours with Dominic after you left Olivia's on Christmas Day? Did you have to eat another lunch like Dawn French? The Vicar's Girlfriend of Hampshire! It's a shame he couldn't join you in Lyndhurst, but that's the downside when you're bonking a man of the cloth. Christmas is a busy time for them.

Now don't forget to remind Dominic to give you my other gift at midnight tonight or whatever time he stops snogging you.

Sending love to you all, but mainly to you because I like you the most.

Happy New Year, my darling friend.

Love Daisy

xxx

To: daisyduke71@gomail.com
From: jane-hubbard@skycorres.co.uk
Date: Saturday, 1st January 01:14

Dear Daisy

I was going to email you tomorrow. But it's tomorrow now. I tried to call you, but your phone was busy.

Let me answer your email first. Christmas was lovely. I had a small lunch with Olivia, Julian, Carrie and the kids and stayed there until around four. They all stayed the night, but I shot back to the vicarage to spend the evening with Dominic. It was such a lovely night. We opened our presents and then just played music and talked and danced and then stayed in bed for most of the following day. Bliss!

I think Julian thought he might hear from his father, but he didn't. Can you believe he's not heard from him since last April? I'm not sure what he would have said to him anyway. He's still pretty angry about it all. To not even say goodbye is disgraceful. He still thinks it's something to do with him, even though Olivia and I have told him it was purely financial, and because of that, he had to leave the country. I don't want to badmouth his father, but I don't want to lie, either. He thinks that's all we know, and that we swooped in and saved the business.

By the way, thanks for sending the papers over. Brendan sorted the final details out, so it's a relief to know that Ben, Julian and Myla are provided for. I love Brendan; he's such a hoot, and he's taught me lots of Liverpudlian sayings that I can try on Jeff. Apparently, I have to say, "Sort your trabs out, mate. They're only fit to be gondolas." I'm told it's a fun way to say his shoes may need an upgrade.

Olivia had six trees. They were all exquisite. I'm not sure how she finds the time, either. She rarely asks me about the business anymore. She's still cooperating with the HMRC about tax and so on. I think she would be lost without Jeff, to be honest. He's been a real rock to her. She said once everything is sorted and cleared, she wants to get him something, A watch, maybe?

Ben is itching to come back to Chorley. I've told him that you're moving, and he asked would he still be able to see Bruno. It was clear that was all he was bothered about.

Anyway, last but not least. My present! Our present! I cannot wait. I need to lose a stone before we go. I've put on so much weight these last few months, as Dominic loves cooking and I can't say no. I hope we have as much fun as we did last time. Can you imagine if the staff remember us? We'll have to sort out our itinerary and what trips we'll take. Have you booked your holidays yet? I'm sure you have. We'll be done with Easter by then, but I'm sure you planned it that way. I'm so excited. Dominic will tell you I was screaming and jumping when he gave me the tickets.

Well, I'm going to go now. I just wanted to send you this so you can read it when you wake. I'll call you later tonight, and we can talk about our cruise!

Night, night, and Happy New Year to the best friend anyone could wish for.

Love Jane

xxx

The
End

Acknowledgements

There are so many people I want to thank for this book.

Let's start with Debbie McGowan, who edited it all to within an inch of its life. Remember Action Man with his eagle eyes? Well, that's Debbie, except she doesn't have a buzz cut or wear camouflage clothing (not really needed in Burscough).

Next are my beta-readers—

Michelle Ewen, who runs a PR firm and can lip-sync better than Milli Vanilli, judging by her hilarious reels on social media, and gave me some valuable advice.

I also want to thank Christie Barlow. She read it with an experienced eye, but I suspect she was full of Taittinger Champagne while reading it. I'm not saying she drinks too much—even I raised an eyebrow when I saw her pouring Veuve Cliquot on her Coco Pops—I'm saying she's loaded.

My third beta-reader was the incredible Lee Gregory. He's always been a fab supporter of my work, but giving it to him in its raw state, I fear, was like trying to 'fold in the cheese' for him. (Sorry if you don't get that reference, readers.)

I would also like to thank Sue Miller and Bob Stone for casting an eye over it and giving me their opinion. And while I'm at it, I'll chuck in Andrea Moulding too. I couldn't stand her begging to read it anymore.

Although they had no part in the production of the book, I want to thank my friends. This book is about friendship, so I feel it necessary to give my own a shout-out. I'm not going to list them all because I'm menopausal and full of brain fog, so I will no doubt forget that one person who will never let me forget it. And knowing my luck, that will be the one who always goes to the bar the most.

Finally, the big thanks go to my family. To my daughter, Chloé, for her unending love and support for absolutely anything and everything I do. She is the person I want to be when I grow up. And to my son, Zack, who helped me pull the story together over a bacon butty. Thanks, Spud.

But the biggest one is to Pete, my Mr M—for the things you do, the things you don't and the things you do when you don't think I notice.

About the Author

Estelle Maher was born in the heart of Liverpool, England. After spending her teens in rural Dorset, she returned to the north of England and now resides in Wirral with her husband, two children and three dogs.

She also writes a blog in her spare time, *The Secret Diary of a Middle-Aged Woman*, a humorous snapshot of random thoughts. The blog was her first step to writing for an audience wider than her and her husband.

Her debut novel, *Grace & The Ghost*, won a Best Spiritual Fiction Award 2018 and her spin-off novel, *Angel's Rebellion*, also became an Amazon bestseller. Her third novel, *The Killing of Tracey Titmass*, is based on her own cancer journey. Told in diary form, it offers an alternative way of depicting cancer. From this, she launched a podcast called *Get It Off Your Chest: The Funny Side of Breast Cancer*. Estelle is now in recovery and still smiles every day.

Website: estellemaher.co.uk

Social Media

Facebook: Estelle Maher Author

Instagram: @estelleauthor

X: @EstelleMaher

TikTok: @estelleauthor

Podcast: Get It Off Your Chest: The Funny Side of Breast Cancer (available on all major podcast and music platforms)

Also by Estelle Maher

Grace & The Ghost

Angel's Rebellion

The Killing of Tracey Titmass

TAUK
Publishing

TAUK Publishing is an established assisted publisher for independent authors in the UK.

With hundreds of titles including novels, non-fiction and children's books, TAUK Publishing is a collaborative-based team providing step-by-step guidance for authors of all genres and formats.

To sign up to our newsletter or submit an enquiry, visit:
https://taukpublishing.co.uk/contact/

For one-to-one advice, consider scheduling a Book Clinic:
https://taukpublishing.co.uk/book-clinic/

Connect with us!

Facebook: @TAUKPublishing
Twitter: @TAUKPublishing
Instagram: @TAUKPublishing
Pinterest: @TAUKPublishing

We love to hear from new or established authors wanting support in navigating the world of self-publishing.
Visit our website for more details on ways we can help you.

https//taukpublishing.co.uk/

SCAN ME

Printed in Great Britain
by Amazon

28923105R00155